Like a Tree

D1596583

Like a Tree

A DAVIS MORGAN MYSTERY

Danny & Wanda Pelfrey

CrossLink Publishing

CrossLink Publishing
13395 Voyager Pkwy, Ste 130
Colorado Springs, CO 80921
www.crosslinkpublishing.com

Ordering Information:
Quantity sales. Special discounts are available on quantity purchases by corporations, associations, and others. For details, contact the "Special Sales Department" at the address above.

Like a Tree/Pelfrey —1st ed.

ISBN 978-1-63357-155-6

Library of Congress Control Number: 2018952433

First edition: 10 9 8 7 6 5 4 3 2 1

CHAPTER 1

Davis Morgan forced himself to keep his eyes on the road with the spring scenes around him so gloriously alive with new growth. It was the kind of late April day that made Davis glad to be resettled into the enchanting North Georgia foothills he had loved as a boy. It occurred to Davis since his brush with death less than five months earlier, courtesy of a severe heart attack, he was now more alert to the simple beauty around him. Though he suspected his trip to Rome would not yield the results he wished for, Davis was at least enjoying the drive back to Adairsville.

As one of only a couple of used and rare book sellers in the area, Davis was always thrilled when asked to evaluate the books left by one of the college town's deceased professors. He enjoyed looking at good books even when it was financially not feasible for him to purchase them. Often the heirs of such an estate had grand ideas about the value of such treasures, forgetting that a dealer, besides making a little profit for himself, has overhead. Davis never compromised his rule for such purchases. If he couldn't purchase the books for less than forty percent of their market value, it was not a worthwhile deal. Today, the sons of Dr. Wilheim reacted to his offer as if he were trying to cheat them out of their inheritance. They finally agreed to think about it and get back to him. Maybe they would contact other sellers and discover that his offer was more than fair, but he wasn't counting on hearing from them anytime soon.

Davis slowed his red Jeep Wrangler before he brought it to a complete halt at the traffic light. He was in no real hurry to get back to Adairsville since Deidre, his young wife of less than eight months would be getting home late due to several parent/ teacher conferences after school. Davis looked at his watch and decided he had time to go by his shop before Janie closed. He hoped to find that some significant sales had been made while he was in Rome. Since his heart attack, Davis no longer had income from the interim ministry he had enjoyed while serving his home church. It was all good though. He was excited about the new man the church called. The first four sermons from the South Carolina native were exceptional, and he seemed to really care about people. Davis felt the committee had done their home-work, enabling them to make a wise decision in calling Clark Jensen to their pulpit.

Davis was now forced to drive cautiously to dodge the con-struction vehicles that seemed to be everywhere. Highway 140 would someday in the future be a four lane. It seemed the process of getting it to that status had been going on forever, but obvi-ously, there was still much to be done before the highway would be completed. When Davis reached downtown Adairsville where his bookshop was housed in the 1902 Stock Exchange building, he was glad to see no trace of the movie company that had been shooting in the downtown area in recent weeks.

Adairsville finally had gotten its share of the state's recent windfall via the region's new-found venture into the motion pic-ture industry. A production company was remaking *THE GREAT LOCOMOTIVE CHASE* as a TV movie. James Andrews and his band of raiders made up of Northern troops had commandeered the General in Big Shanty, now known as Kennesaw, just forty miles south of Adairsville. The chase took place on the very railroad bed now running through town. It was the same 1845 train depot at which Davis was presently looking as he turned his head to the west that Andrews and his raiders saw in 1862. The earlier Disney movie portraying the same event had been shot in the nineteen fifties sixty miles east of Adairsville, but when

producers were considering sites for this remake, they were immediately drawn to Adairsville with its original depot and restored business section. The citizens of Adairsville were, for the
most part, pleased with the decision but were now finding the
bottlenecking it sometimes created a little disconcerting.

Davis was lucky enough to find a parking space almost in front
of the large building where his bookshop and several other shops
were located along with a tearoom and an upstairs theater where
patrons regularly congregated for dinner theater productions. He
took his cell phone from his pocket before getting out of the car.
Amy, his daughter, who also taught at Adairsville High, had no
after school commitments, as far as he knew, and would probably
be home by now. He punched the button that would connect him
to her and heard the phone ring three times before he recognized
the voice of his only offspring.

"Hello Dad, what are you up to?"

"I've just returned to the shop from Rome and thought I would
call to see how your day has been."

"My day has been fine, Dad. I know I'm seven months pregnant and look like an elephant, but you don't have to constantly
call to check on me. Millions of ladies have successfully had ba-
bies. It's all very normal," she reminded her father. "I think you
are more worried about this than Jay," she added.

"I know millions of women have given birth, but they weren't
my only daughter. There is no doubt in my mind you are going to
be fine but let me suggest that you need to sit down and put your
feet up for a while."

"Dad, remember, I've got a husband, and he will need his dinner when he gets home in an hour or so. I'll get it started. He'll
help me when he gets home after which we'll have a nice, peaceful meal. I will then sit down, put my feet up and grade some
papers while he cleans up."

"Okay, but make sure you take care of yourself."

"I could say the same to you. You're the one who had what was almost a fatal heart attack a few months ago. Are you monitoring your meals as the doctor instructed? I know how much you like red meat," Amy declared.

"I'm eating great," Davis told his daughter.

"That's what I'm afraid of," the sassy young lady replied.

"I'll call you in the next day or two." Davis was suddenly anxious to get off the phone. "I love you, good-bye."

When he walked inside, Davis found Janie, the young clerk at the 1902 Stock Exchange checking out two customers. He was disappointed when he saw their purchases were not from his shop. "How's it gone today?" Davis addressed the attractive young lady behind the counter after the customers left.

"It's gone well for some of the shops. We've had lots of customers, but I'm afraid I haven't sold a thing for you."

"I was afraid of that. Janie, you've got to work harder. Remember, I now have a wife to support." Davis teased the gregarious young clerk with the long auburn hair.

"I can't help it if nobody wants your dusty old books. Some things are just impossible to sell, no matter how good the sales person." Janie directed her thoughts to Davis with her strong southern accent and then stuck her tongue out at him.

"How are you and what's his name, the big movie man, getting along these days?" Davis inquired.

"His name is Devan Rhodes, and he's not a movie man. He's a site director. It's his job to find the right place for each scene, negotiate it's use, and then set it up appropriately," she corrected.

"Then how are you and Mr. Rhodes, the site director guy, getting along these days?" Davis asked.

"We're getting along fantastically. He's definitely awesome sauce," Janie told her friend while giggling.

"Awesome sauce. What does that mean?" Davis asked and then added, "Sounds like he's on the menu."

"I forgot I was talking to an old fogy or maybe I should be more politically correct and say an older gentleman." Janie who loved to harass Davis about his age replied. "It means he's cool, hip, groovy, sophisticated. You might understand better if I told you he's the cat's meow."

"Now I'm insulted," Davis informed his co-worker with a hint of a laugh. "I may have a few years on me, but I don't go back that far."

"We've had several dates, and I like him a whole lot. In fact, we're planning to go to dinner in Marietta tonight. He was to call me this afternoon about time and such, but I haven't heard a word from him. I've tried to call him several times, but the calls just go to message, and he has returned none of those calls. He was going out to Spring Bank to survey it for possible use in a scene. Actually, I am a little concerned about him."

"It's probably nothing to worry about. He most likely got busy and hasn't had time to return your calls." Davis tried to reassure her.

"Maybe," Janie responded. "But in the past when I called him, he either picked up or returned my call almost immediately. I was thinking about going out there to check on him, but then I remembered Mom took my car this morning and I walked to work. She won't be home for another couple of hours."

"Would you like me to drive you there?" Davis asked.

"I can't ask you to do that. Deidre is probably home waiting for you."

"She has parent/teacher conferences today and won't be home for a while yet. Lock up and we can be there in ten or twelve minutes," Davis instructed.

They were soon in Davis's Jeep traveling toward Kingston. Have you ever been to the Spring Bank site?" Davis asked his passenger.

"No, I haven't," Janie answered. "But I've noticed the historical signs beside the road and stone structural remains on the opposite side when I passed by on my way to Kingston. I used to go out that way a lot since I have family living there. I've heard people mention Spring Bank often, but I don't know much about it."

"Let me give you a little history," Davis responded. "Everyone needs to know about the past of their home area."

"Oh boy, just what I wanted, a history lesson. Okay, give me the facts and try not to bore me to tears."

"Well, Spring Bank was the name Charles Wallace Howard gave his almost thousand-acre plantation when he came here from Savannah around 1850. It was a successful working plantation with a boy's school where many boys from far and near were educated, as well as the Howard girls. Those same girls later converted it to a girl's school. Natural ingredients for cement were discovered across the road after the Civil War, which made it possible to establish the Howard Hydraulic Cement Company. With the train tracks running right through the business location, for many years cement was shipped all over the country. The success of that company led to a small town of approximately one hundred people rising on that site. It was called Cement, Georgia, and had a school, post office and church. The town disappeared in the early twentieth century when the company ceased to be productive. The stone ruins you mentioned earlier are all that remain of what was once an extremely profitable concern. The plantation house across the highway beside the spring remained until it, in terrible condition, burned down maybe fifty years ago."

Davis lifted his foot off the accelerator and tapped the brake when he saw two cows grazing on the side of the road. "Looks like some farmer needs to do some fence repair," Davis suggested and slowed to slightly more than a stop as he passed the cows.

"I know why you slowed down; It wasn't your concern for the cows. You were afraid a collision with a cow would dent your Jeep," Janie accused.

"You're partly right," Davis told her. "I wouldn't want to hurt a cow, but I don't want any dents on my Jeep either. There's a lot more interesting history about Spring Bank, especially Civil War history, that I'll share with you another time," he told her knowing they were near their destination.

"I can hardly wait for that," Janie sarcastically responded.

"It really is a beautiful spot. The county maintains about forty acres as a green space. The rest of what was once plantation fields and woods is part of the hunting reserve of the Barnsley Gardens Resort," Davis informed her.

After turning right on an unpaved road and driving about a hundred yards, they spotted a parked car. "That's Devan's rental," Janie informed Davis. They got out of the Jeep but saw no one. After a few moments Janie called out. "Devan, where are you?" There was no answer.

"He's probably at the Howard family cemetery or the big oak tree. The state champion white oak is just a couple hundred yards over that way" Davis pointed southeast as he spoke. "It's probably three hundred years old and huge," he told her. "If they were to shoot out here, I'm sure they would want to include it."

The two friends heard gun shots as they walked in the direction Davis had pointed. "What's that?" Janie asked turning her face in the direction of the shots.

"That's people over on the Barnsley hunting reserve, probably shooting at birds or maybe skeet shooting," he informed her. Seeing the large tree up ahead, Davis pointed in its direction.

"There it is. Isn't it incredible?"

"What's that beside the tree?" Janie asked with a note of panic in her voice.

A quick glance told Davis all was not right. There was a person, a man on the ground sprawled on his back. A closer look told him that the large spot on his powder blue shirt in the chest area could be blood.

At that moment the scene registered with Janie, and she began to run toward the downed figure beside the tree screaming, "Devan, Devan, help him Davis, he's hurt."

Davis tried to catch the horrified young lady to stop her before she reached her destination, but she had too much of a head start on him and was on her knees beside the bloody body sobbing by the time he reached her.

CHAPTER 2

D espite her resistance, Davis was able to pull Janie to her feet and station her a few steps away from the lifeless body on the ground. He returned to the bloody form and stooped to check the pulse. There was no doubt about it. They could do nothing for Devan. He was gone. Davis stood to his feet, took his cell from his pocket and punched the button for 911. "This is Davis Morgan. A few moments ago, we found a body under the big oak tree at the Spring Bank green space near Kingston. You need to get someone out here as soon as possible."

Upon hearing Davis's words, Janie's sobs turned to what was almost hysterical shrieks. Davis quickly moved to embrace her and tried to comfort the distraught young woman while at the same time attempting to answer the questions of the 911 operator.

In fewer than fifteen minutes, there were several people, including four Bartow County sheriff's deputies, swarming all over the green space. The body was placed in an ambulance causing Janie, who a little earlier had become silent, to again break into loud sobs. After successfully calming her a bit, Davis placed Janie in the passenger seat of his Jeep. He closed the door, but after walking around to the other side, he removed his cell from his pocket and called Deidre who answered right away.

"You'll never guess what happened!" Davis told his wife.

There were a few seconds of silence before Deidre responded. "From the tone of your voice, I'm almost afraid to ask. What happened?"

"I drove Janie out to Spring Bank to check on her boyfriend, the guy with the movie company. To get right to the point, when we got here, we found him dead—shot I think."

"Oh Davis, that's horrible! How's Janie?"

"As you might expect, she's inconsolable, in shock perhaps." Knowing she had to be dead tired, Davis was a little reluctant to ask for his wife's help, but he did so anyway. "Deidre, we're leaving now and should be back to Adairsville in ten or twelve minutes. I hate to ask you, but could you meet us at Janie's house? I think you can do more for her now than I can."

"Sure, Honey, you didn't have to ask. Janie is my friend too. I should be in her driveway before you get there."

As often happens, the thought regarding how fortunate he was to have a wife like Deidre ran through Davis's mind. After Julie became a fatal victim of cancer, Davis thought he could never be totally happy again, but here he was nine months after his marriage to Deidre with just about everything a man could want. Deidre would soon celebrate her thirtieth birthday, and he was already in his late forties. There were those that feared the seventeen years between his and her ages would surely create barriers, but so far there had been none, and at this point, he didn't expect that would ever happen.

Janie was quiet with her face in her hands when they turned left onto Hall Station Road to start the drive back to Adairsville. Davis took advantage of the time of calmness to silently pray for his young friend in the seat beside him. Earlier today she had been in a jovial mood, laughing and joking with just about everyone with whom she came in contact. Now, her world was turned upside down. He remembered being there not so long ago, and he longed to somehow take away her pain.

***

Charley Nelson and his date Tonya Willis, together, had devoured most of the food served them by Cynthia, their efficient waitress at the Adairsville Inn, but it was Charley who did most of the damage. Tonya had pretty much been Charley's steady date for the past four months. He was mindful that this fact amazed a lot of people around town who knew him well. In the past, the young Adairsville policeman had played the field, and there seemed always to be an attractive young lady willing to take a stab at taming one of the town's most eligible bachelors. None had done so until the sweet, dark-headed pint of an EMT got Charley's attention, first earning his respect, and then, it appeared, his affection.

It seemed to Charley though, that this evening she was different than the girl with whom he thought he was falling in love. She was quieter than usual. And her eyes, those eyes that usually sparkled with life, were dull tonight. The girl who typically smiled non-stop wasn't smiling at all, and Charley missed that smile. He finally laid his fork on the table and looked directly into his dates brown eyes. "Obviously there's something wrong, Tonya. Is it something I did?"

There was a moment of silence that seemed to Charley to last for five minutes. Eventually Tonya responded. "No, my dear Charley, it's nothing you've done. It's something I'm about to do. I have been sitting here all evening trying to figure out how to tell you."

Panic gripped Charley as Tonya spoke slowly, glancing away and then back at him. "You remember me telling you about the death of my brother Edward's wife earlier last year. You'll remember that Edward lives in Jacksonville, Florida, and has three children, all under eight. He's trying his best not only to keep them together as a family, but to provide a degree of normalcy to their existence. He's not well off financially, so he's often working ten hours a day, six days a week just to pay the bills. Charley, he needs my help. With my injuries in that accident late last year, I've already put it off too long. I've decided to move to Jacksonville to do my part. I don't know what else I can do."

Charley was speechless at first. Finally, he responded with the only thing he could think to say, "I know how much you enjoy your work as an EMT. Are you going to be happy without that?" The voice of the stunned young officer was barely loud enough to be heard.

"That's all worked out," Tonya replied. "My boss here in Bartow county made the contact in Jacksonville that netted me a job that will enable me to do the work I love doing for three days and then be off for three days. It's not a perfect setup, but I'll have at least three full days out of every week to be a substitute mother to those three girls."

"You've already worked all this out and never even talked with me about it?" Charley questioned, obviously disappointed. "I thought we were close enough that you would at least let me know what you were thinking."

"I wanted too, Charley, and almost did several times, but I just couldn't. You're so special to me, and I couldn't bring myself to hurt you, and I think I was also holding on to hope that something would come along to change the whole situation. It's not something I want to do, but something I feel I must do," Tonya explained.

"Where does that leave us?" Charley barked, now disturbed that he had been left out of this altogether. He wanted to tell her that he was ready to get on his knees and ask her to spend the rest of her life with him. He wanted to tell her that he had been dreaming of taking her shopping for a ring, but none of that seemed appropriate now.

"I guess it sort of puts us on hold," She told the disappointed love of her life. "It's not fair for me to ask you to sit around here and wait to see how things ultimately work out with me. You have told me more than once that you love me, and I certainly love you with all my heart, but love doesn't always get its way.

Who knows what the future holds, but as much as I hate it, for now we're just going to have to get on with our lives without the joy of one another's frequent company."

"If I'm reading you right, you're telling me that you're not closing the door on our relationship, but for now we're both free to date other people."

"It's really no different than it's always been with us. Even though the past few months we've chosen to see each other exclusively, neither of us has ever suggested it had to be that way. So, nothing's really changed," Tonya surmised.

But to Charley, it seemed that everything had changed. "I wish I could be more understanding, and maybe that'll be possible in a few days, but right now I'm disappointed and a little upset about the whole situation," Charley related to her on their way to her little house in the small community of White. Reaching their destination, Charley walked her to the door where he pecked her on the cheek before he muttered, "goodnight" and turned to walk back to his car.

Tonya with a sad look on her face stood at the door. She watched him all the way to the car. She didn't go inside and close the door until he drove completely out of sight.

Instead of turning north towards Adairsville when he got to Highway 75, Charley steered the car south in the direction of Cartersville. He hadn't had a drink of alcohol in any form in over nine months, but tonight he felt the need for a drink or two. He didn't feel much like going to a bar, but he knew where to get the strong stuff that he could take home with him.

***

Davis and Deidre remained with Janie for a time, waiting until her mother got home. Deidre had the kind of comforting effect on the young woman that Davis had presumed she would. "I think I was falling in love with him," Janie told them. "Recently

I've been telling myself that he was the one. I've never even met any of his family."

"Where's he from Janie? Where does his family live?" Davis inquired.

"I'm not even sure where he's originally from. I know he has lived in both North and South Carolina and for a few months in California. He's worked in the movie industry since college, and most of his close friends also work in that field in some capacity."

"Who seemed to be the people closest to him with the company working here in Adairsville?" Davis asked.

"He spent a lot of time with a man named Max. Right now, I can't remember his full name. I can't think of anyone else he talked about. There may have been someone, but I'm just not thinking clearly right now," Janie said, again starting to whimper.

Deidre placed her arm around the shoulder of the grieving young woman beside her on the sofa. "We understand, Janie. You don't have to talk unless you want to," she assured her.

After Mrs. Edison returned and took charge of her daughter, Davis and Deidre drove their respective vehicles back to their house three or four minutes away. Davis noticed there were no lights on the south side of the house where their renter, Barbara Mason lived in the apartment once occupied by Deidre and Amy when both were still single. Barbara, also a teacher and a long-time friend of Deidre's took Amy's spot when she moved out. After Deidre and Davis were married, Barbara, at first, had a roommate by the name of Randi, but that didn't work out well; however, Barbara as the only occupant was a good arrangement. They would probably maintain that situation until Barbara, who would retire in two years, decided to move back to South Georgia where other members of her family lived. It was Davis's plan to then convert his old homeplace back to a one-family dwelling.

Both Davis and Deidre were out of their vehicles walking side by side, but not yet to the big front porch when Davis remembered they hadn't yet eaten dinner. "Why don't we go to one of the restaurants out on the highway and get something to eat," he suggested to his wife.

"Sounds like a winner to me." Deidre spoke with a voice that gave evidence of the long day she had endured. Together they turned back toward the red Jeep.

CHAPTER 3

Disturbed by the events of the previous day, Davis got little sleep, but tried not to toss and turn. He knew Deidre, who would be in her classroom throughout the coming day, needed some rest. When morning came, he waited until his wife took her shower before getting out of bed. Deidre prepared breakfast while he shaved and showered, then they sat down together at the table for a bowl of oatmeal, which had been his most frequent breakfast staple since his heart attack.

Deidre remained uncommonly quiet, causing Davis to think something was on her mind. Ultimately, she spoke her piece as Davis knew she would. "Honey, there's something I want to say to you, and I promise you I'll speak of it only this once. I don't want to be a nag, but I know you have a special knack for solving crimes like what happened to Janie's friend yesterday. I know it's possible you could help catch whoever was responsible for that poor man's death," she continued. "But you know what your doctor said about your heart. Your heart isn't going to stand a lot of stress. So please, let the authorities handle this one." She pleaded with a serious expression on her face. "Don't get involved."

"Well, Sweetheart, since I found the body, I guess I can't help but be involved a little bit. But you don't have to worry. Since the corpse was found near Kingston, this will be under the jurisdiction of the Bartow County Sheriff's Office. Charley and the boys will have little to do with this investigation, which means I'll be completely out of the loop. I'll try to be of help to Janie, and I do want to follow the case from a distance, but I don't intend to take an active role. But please remember what the doctor said about my heart when I had my checkup last week. Everything looks good. You don't have to worry about me."

"I know that, but I just needed to get my two cents worth in," Deidre told him. "You know how much I love you. I don't want anything to happen to you. I need you," she added with a stern glance his way that was followed by one of her sweet smiles.

Pam, a middle-aged lady who sometimes subbed for Janie, was at the cash register when Davis got to the shop. After a smile and a quick greeting, Davis walked to the back of the building where his shop was located. He did some straightening up. It always amazed him how out of order a bookshop can get even when there hasn't been a lot of browsers.

After a few minutes of busy work Davis returned to the front checkout counter. "If anyone comes looking for me, Pam, tell them I'll be back shortly. I'm going to walk down the street for a short visit," he told the lady holding down the fort. The Police Station was just one block away. Perhaps he would find Charley there, and they could talk over the events of the previous day.

Chief Hanson was standing in the middle of the small hall-way with a file folder in his hand when Davis walked through the door. "I believe it's the chaplain himself." Hanson spoke with a smile on his face as he moved the folder from his right hand to his left to extend the proper hand to Davis. "How's the old ticker doing," he inquired. "I hear you had quite an experience yesterday."

"The doctor tells me everything's all right with the heart, and yes I did happen upon a bad situation late yesterday afternoon." Davis had gotten to know Chief Hanson well over the past year or so. He, a former pastor, had served as chaplain to the department during those months.

"What can I do for you Davis?" The uniformed policeman asked.

"I was wondering if Charley is around, and if so, could I speak to him for a moment?"

"Charley's not here today. I don't remember him ever calling in sick before, but he did this morning. I gave him the day off," Chief Hanson explained.

"I keep hearing rumors that you're just about ready to retire. Any truth to those?" Davis asked.

"Having grown up around here, I thought you knew by now not to pay any attention to the gossip floating about. I've given it a little thought though. All three of my children are grown and scattered. Not one of them lives within a hundred miles of here. I inherited a small farm located near Commerce that's sitting vacant. I think I would like to spend some time on an old John Deere tractor or maybe feeding a few head of cattle, but I don't know if I'm ready for that yet."

"I understand," Davis remarked. "I guess the presence of the movie company is keeping you guys hopping."

"You bet it is!" The Chief responded almost before Davis finished his statement. "One of their big shots, a man named Max Tobias, reported to us this morning that someone broke into his motel room last night leaving a real mess."

Davis remembered that Janie had mentioned that Devan's friend was called Max. "Did the intruders take anything?" Davis inquired.

"Not that we could tell. Fortunately, I guess Mr. Tobias had not left anything of value there while he was out. I understand Mr. Rhodes's room had also been rummaged through. If this keeps up, Davis, I may have to give you a badge," the chief added.

"That would be a sure way to put me in the dog house with both my wife and my daughter." Davis responded with a short laugh.

After a brief chat with Chief Hanson, Davis headed back toward the shop but decided to stop and give Charley a call. He pulled his cell phone from his pocket and took a seat on one of the benches in front of a store. Charley didn't answer, and it soon went to message, "Charley, this is Davis. Just checking on you. Give me a call."

Davis was able to temporarily postpone the work waiting for him down the street by stopping in at the General Store & Mercantile to say good morning to his friend Carol and her daughter. Carol, as always, had a smile for him, but she was busy, and he didn't want to hinder her work, so he proceeded on down the street.

Pam was standing at the same spot where he left her thirty minutes earlier, behind the checkout station. "There's a gentleman waiting for you in your shop," she announced rather formally.

Davis picked up his pace as he headed for his corner. When he got to the bookshop, he found a man a little older than himself in overalls, a plaid shirt, and a green John Deere cap nonchalantly examining the books on one of the history shelves. "I'm Davis Morgan. Can I help you sir?" Davis inquired.

"Yes sir, I'm Douglas Touchstone. I understand you're the one who found that man dead out near Kingston yesterday."

"That's right. It was me and a young lady," Davis answered.

The gentleman glanced at Davis a little suspiciously.

"She's the clerk here, and I took her out there to help her find her boyfriend, who turned out to be the deceased," Davis quickly explained.

"Well, I live out that way and run a few head of cattle. Yesterday I had a fence down and was out in my pickup looking for several of my cows that had wandered away."

"Yes, I think I saw a couple head of your livestock," Davis told him.

"I eventually got all of them back in the pasture, but while I was searching, I drove into the Spring Bank green space to see if they had perhaps roamed in that direction. I didn't find any cattle there, but on the way in I saw an odd-looking man leaving in an old car."

"What time was that Mr. Touchstone?" Davis questioned.

"I don't know exactly, but it must've been around a quarter till five."

"You said he was an odd-looking man, can you describe him for me?" Davis continued to probe.

"Yes, I got a pretty good look at him because that's a narrow little road, and when we met, we both had to almost stop. He had long curly red hair. I mean it was long. I think maybe below his shoulders. He had long bushy sideburns and a mustache that turned downward. His face was sort of white like he had not gotten a lot of sun. I'll tell you what came to mind when I saw him." The farmer was talking slower now as if a little reluctant to share his observation. "A few nights back, we watched that movie on TV. You know the one, The Wizard of Oz. He looked like the Cowardly Lion." Mr. Touchstone revealed with a silly little grin on his face.

"That's a pretty detailed description Mr. Touchstone."

"Call me Doug, Mr. Morgan. Everybody does."

"I'll do that, and I want you to call me Davis. Can you tell me about the car this man was driving?"

"Like I said earlier, it was an old car. I don't recognize makes and models very well, but it was a black car that had to be at least ten or twelve years old. I noticed it badly needed to be washed."

"Doug, I appreciate you coming by. You've been extremely helpful. You need to call the Bartow County Sheriff's Department and tell them everything you've told me as well as anything else that comes to your mind later. They are handling the investigation, and what you can tell them may very well be the key to their finding the murderer." Davis told his new friend.

"Let me ask one thing before I go. Do you think that man was dead out there under that tree when I drove into that layout and got out of my truck to look around for my cows?" Douglas asked.

"It would seem to me that indeed he was. If you had arrived five minutes earlier, your own life might have been in jeopardy. You are a blessed man, Doug."

"I'll be! That never occurred to me. You never know what you're going to walk into do you?"

Davis decided not to leave the building at lunch time. He ate a Reuben sandwich and some chips ordered from Maggie Mae's Tea Room there in the 1902 Stock Exchange. He kept waiting for Charlie to return his call. He desperately wanted to discuss yesterday's events with him. *Charley must be seriously ill, otherwise he would be all over this. This is right down his alley even if he's not involved in the official investigation.* Davis took some time to silently pray for his friend but regretted not having any idea about how to specifically pray. He made the decision to go by Charley's apartment in the middle of the afternoon if he hadn't heard anything from him by then.

It was a blessing to Davis's pocket book that several people came in to buy books over the next couple of hours. The sale of a first edition copy of Grisham's *A Time to Kill* made it a profitable afternoon. It wasn't a perfect copy, but still somewhat valuable due to its being a very small printing from a small publishing house. Davis dropped the price a little for the customer, but still got almost five hundred dollars for a book he took off a thrift store shelf for two dollars.

The other sales were less significant— of the nine and ten-dollar variety, but the beauty of it was that the small sales all add up. It was those sales that, in the long run, gave him most of his profit, but it was good to occasionally move something from the high end of his inventory. Davis had loved books for most of his life, but he was just now learning the business end of his recently chosen profession. Sometimes he longed to return to the pastorate.

CHAPTER 4

It was close to three-thirty when Davis got into his Jeep to drive the short distance to Charley's apartment. When he drove past the police station, Davis noticed two Bartow County Sheriff's Department patrol cars in parking spaces in front of the building. *I suppose that'll be a regular occurrence until Devan's murder is solved*, he guessed.

When Davis parked his Jeep and started up the walkway toward the apartment where Charley lived, he met two boys with baseball mitts understandably excited after having just gotten home from being cooped up at school all day. He greeted the boys. "Hi, guys. I wish I could take the time to play some ball with you fellas." They looked at him strangely. He rang Charley's doorbell without getting a response. After two or three minutes, he rang it a second time—still no Charley. Davis turned to look at the car parked on the street to make sure it was indeed Charley's car. It was definitely Charley's pride and joy. *Maybe he's asleep*, Davis speculated. He once again stepped forward to the door and rang the bell again, this time calling out, "Charley, it's Davis. I need to see you."

After a minute or two the door opened. Charley looked terrible, squinting and shading his eyes with his right hand as if the sun light were blinding him. *He must really be sick*, Davis thought. Then he caught a whiff of an odor that immediately gave away Charley's problem. Davis's heart sank. There was no missing the strong stench of liquor. Charley's living room reeked of it.

"I thought if I waited long enough you'd go away, but you can't take a hint, can you?" Charley grumbled.

"I bet you did, Charley, what's this all about?" Davis's voice gave evidence of both disappointment and concern.

"It's a long story that you don't want to hear." Charley turned to walk back into the living room allowing himself to collapse onto the couch while motioning for Davis's benefit toward a chair. "Take a seat." He talked as if it hurt him to speak

"You had anything to eat today?" Davis asked.

"I don't want anything to eat. "I don't know of anything I could keep down," the hungover young policeman told his friend.

"Well, you have to try. I'm going into your kitchen to make some coffee and see if I can find something to make a sandwich for you."

"You're getting pretty bossy in your old age, aren't you?" Charley asked.

"Only when the situation demands it," Davis responded.

Davis prepared the coffee maker and then went to the refrigerator to find luncheon meat, mayonnaise, and mustard. He put the ingredients between two slices of bread and cut it before serving it to Charley. Davis then went back into the kitchen to pour a cup of the freshly brewed coffee for his friend. When he returned with the cup in his hand, it looked like Charley had taken one bite of the sandwich before putting it on the table beside the sofa. "You drink that cup, and I'll get you another," he told the obviously miserable Charley.

"I know you've been on the wagon for months. It must've been something serious to cause you to get smashed like this. Are you ready to talk about it?"

"I hadn't had a single drink since before I took that bullet back in December and very little for three months before that. I guess when I did jump off the wagon, I really did it up right. I don't think I've been this plastered since I was a teenager, and Dad gave me a lecture I thought I would never forget."

"You apparently did forget," Davis countered. "And I guess now that you drank half the liquor in Bartow County, everything is all right again?"

"I don't think I've ever heard you be so sarcastic, Preacher," Charley retorted, emphasizing the word *preacher*.

"I don't think I've ever been this disappointed in you," Davis scolded. "You are a far bigger person than this."

"I thought I was too, but maybe not." Charley dropped his head and kept his eyes focused on the floor. "Maybe I'm not as big a person as either of us thought."

"Well, one mistake doesn't make one a bad person. The test is how we handle that mistake. Do we let it keep us down, or do we get up and go on from there with more determination than before? I'm not going to preach to you, but I believe you're the kind of man who'll put this behind you and get on with it." Davis smiled at his young friend and picked up the sandwich, handing it to Charley, "Come on, I went through all the trouble to make this for you, the least you can do is eat it."

Charley took a couple of bites before he again placed the sandwich on the table. "It's Tonya," he told Davis. "I thought she was the one. I was ready to set a date. I'm tired of living my life all alone. She's the only unattached woman I've found that I can honestly see tying myself down with for the rest of my life."

"Then what's the problem?" Davis asked. "Ask her to marry you. You're an outgoing sort of guy who shouldn't have a problem with that."

"No, I wouldn't have any difficulty in proposing if she were available."

"What do you mean by that? The last time I checked she lived over near White."

"That's where she lives today, but shortly she'll be living in Florida. She's taken a job in Jacksonville and plans to move in with her brother, whose wife died last fall, to help take care of his three girls."

"That's just the kind of thing you would expect of Tonya. It's one of the factors that makes her so special," Davis declared. "She cares about people and that's a good thing."

"Is this arrangement with her brother's family to be a permanent thing?" Davis asked.

"I don't think so. I was so upset when she told me that I didn't ask a lot of questions."

"Jacksonville is not that far away and after all you have your pilot's license. You two should be able to get together on a regular basis. Jacksonville would be a neat place to hang out, especially with someone you love. You do love her, don't you?"

"Of course, I do. I wouldn't be so upset if I didn't." Charley's tone revealed his displeasure with Davis questioning his love for the girl he had dated for several months and adored.

"Then why are you being so selfish regarding her? She's attempting to help her brother with a serious problem, and you're so upset about how it affects you that you go out and get tanked. In my book that's pure, unadulterated selfishness."

"You said you weren't going to preach me a sermon. Sounds to me like you've got a pretty good one going here," Charley accused.

"After spending all those years in the pulpit, you don't expect me to cut it off just like that, do you?"

"I guess not, and maybe there's a little truth to what you're saying. I'll talk with Tonya and see what comes of it."

Davis was thinking, *that's what he should've done in the first place instead of trying to solve it with a bottle.* But instead of saying what he was thinking, he declared, "That's great. It's surprising how many of our problems can be solved if we take time to talk with each other about them. When is Tonya planning to leave for Jacksonville?" Davis asked.

"I don't know," Charley responded. "I don't think she told me."

"Then you'd better call her and arrange a time for that talk right away."

"I guess so, I'll give her a call as soon as you leave."

"Before I leave, there's one more thing I want to bounce off you. Have you heard about what Janie and I ran into yesterday?" Davis questioned.

"The chief mentioned something about that when I called in early this morning, but I'd just about forgotten about it. Did he say you and Janie found her boyfriend dead?"

"That's pretty much it in a nutshell. Late yesterday afternoon, I took Janie to Spring Bank looking for Devan, her friend from the movie company. We found him dead under the big oak tree, seemingly from a gunshot."

"Any ideas about who did it?" Charley asked.

"Not a clue," Davis responded. Then he corrected himself. "There was a farmer looking for his cattle who saw a weird-looking, red-headed man who he said looked like the Cowardly Lion from the *Wizard of Oz* leaving that area, evidently shortly after the murder."

"The Cowardly Lion!" Charley responded in surprise. "What made him look like the Cowardly Lion?"

"Oh, Mr. Touchstone recently saw the movie and thought the man's curly red hair below his shoulders, bushy side burns, a turned down type of mustache with light complexion made him look like the lion."

"He shouldn't be hard to find. There probably aren't a lot of people fitting that description walking around here," Charley declared.

"You say that, but how long did it take us to apprehend the Rat-Face Man and String Bean and the Sumo Wrestler? They all have distinctive looks, but were not so easy to latch onto," Davis reminded Charley.

"I'm sure the Sheriff's handling it, but I don't think he will mind me nosing around a little in my spare time. Sounds like an interesting case," Charley stated. "How's Janie doing?" he asked.

Davis was glad to observe that Charley was starting to take an interest in something other than his own problem. "She's badly shaken," Davis answered, but I'm sure with the help of those of us who love her, she'll get through it. While you are nosing around, see what you can find out about Devan Rhodes's past. Janie felt exceptionally close to him but knew very little about his past."

"You told me you were through playing detective. I knew you couldn't do it," Charley mocked.

"I'm not playing detective. I'm just curious," Davis assured him.

"Is that what it is? You know what they say about curiosity? Why don't you admit it? There's no way you can stay away from a serious mystery," Charley declared.

"Believe what you want, but I'm through with that. No more stalking around in dark alleys looking for bad guys."

"If you say so," Charley scoffed.

"Eat your sandwich. I'll go get you another cup of coffee." Davis told Charley trying to change the subject.

"Go on home to your wife and stop acting like a mother hen. I can get my own coffee."

"I will if you promise me you'll stay away from the liquor after I leave," Davis told him.

"It'll be easy enough to stay away from since there is none left. I drank both bottles," he explained. "I don't think I could make it to the store for another purchase, and I'm not sure my head could survive more anyway. I feel terrible!"

"Good, you ought to. A man who would drink two bottles overnight doesn't deserve a lot of sympathy. What you feel is all self-inflicted." Davis spoke sternly.

"I always had you pegged for a man with a lot of compassion, but that's not what I'm hearing now."

"Just a little tough love," Davis explained.

At that moment Davis's telephone rang. "Hello," he answered after pulling it from his pocket.

"Davis, this is Janie." There was panic in her voice. "You've got to get over here right away. We need your help quickly."

"I'm at Charley's and can be there in about three minutes," Davis informed her before putting the phone back in his pocket.

"Got to go, Charley. That was Janie. Seems she's in trouble."

"I'll be right behind you," Charley announced.

"You stay where you are. You're not in any condition to be out."

"I just need to wash my face, and I'll be all right."

"You need to wash more than your face. I've got to go," Davis said before going through the door and heading toward his Jeep at a pace that could be called a slow trot.

CHAPTER 5

When Davis got to Janie's house, she and her mother, Rita Edison, were standing in the front yard with worried looks on their faces. "Someone has been in the house," Janie called out. She briskly headed toward Davis as he got out of his vehicle. "We locked the door when we left a little more than an hour ago," she explained. "When we returned, as you can see," she pointed toward the front door, "it's open."

From his vantage point, Davis observed that the door was slightly ajar. "Have you been inside yet?" Davis asked.

"Are you kidding,?" Janie excitedly countered. "That's why we called you. We aren't about to go in there without the help of reinforcements."

"Let's check it out." Davis suggested.

"Mom and I will be right behind you. You lead the way."

"Are you sure you locked the door when you left," Davis asked.

"Absolutely, I remember very clearly locking it and then turning the bolt to guarantee it was secure."

"The first thing we need to do is make sure no one is still in there," Davis declared.

"I think we'll wait here on the porch." Janie's attitude about following Davis into the house had suddenly changed.

"I'm not going to wait here," Rita declared. "I'm going in and getting my pistol."

"You're going to stay out here on the porch with me while Davis checks things out," her daughter asserted. "You need to stay away from that old gun. You're going to end up accidently shooting yourself or someone else. I thought I told you weeks ago to get rid of that thing."

"Then how will we defend ourselves. We'll end up like your boyfriend. I know how to use a gun," Mrs. Edison assured her daughter.

"It doesn't matter," Janie told her. "Davis can look through the house without our help."

The moment Davis walked through the front door, he knew the house had been searched. Someone was looking for something. As he walked through the various rooms of the small dwelling, he saw that almost everything that was supposed to be closed was open, drawers, cabinet doors, and even closet doors. In some cases, the contents had been dumped on the floor or onto a piece of furniture.

After Davis was sure there was no one in the house, he called to Janie and her mother. "Come on in. The coast is clear."

Mrs. Edison gasped when she saw the disheveled condition of her living room. "What happened here?"

"It's like this throughout the house. Your visitor was looking for something and didn't bother to clean up after himself," Davis told the mother and daughter. "Janie you had better call the police and get them out here."

"Mrs. Edison, you mentioned that you own a gun. Would you check to see if it's where you left it? Don't touch it but check to see if it's still where you last put it."

Rita went into the kitchen, pulled out a small folding ladder, perhaps three-feet-high, and climbed to the top rung to enable her to reach to the back of one of the top shelves. She nodded her head as she got off the ladder. "It's still there," she reported.

Even though Davis counted Janie among his closest friends, he didn't know Mrs. Edison very well. About all he knew about her was that she had outlived two husbands, Janie's father who had passed away when Janie was in her early teens and Jack Edison who died of a heart attack only four years after their marriage.

He knew that Rita leaned heavily on Janie and sometimes her demands could make Janie's life a little difficult.

Davis, while caught up in his thoughts, was mildly startled by the ringing of his cell phone in his pocket. He looked at the number on the screen and saw that it was Charley. "Yes Charley," he answered.

"Is everything all right out there? When I was getting ready I got nauseated and a little dizzy. If you need me, I'm sure I can make it, but if you don't, I'm going to rest so I'll be ready for work tomorrow."

"We're fine," Davis told his out-of-sorts friend. "Evidently, someone broke into the house while Janie and her mother were away, but I'm with them now, and the boys in uniform are on the way. You get your rest, so you can go in and do your job tomorrow."

"Okay," Charley responded and was gone. That sudden approach that Charley often used in ending a call usually irritated Davis but not today. He really didn't want to talk with Charley right now. That was partly due to his being extremely disappointed in his best friend but also because he needed to give his attention to the state of affairs where he was.

Chief Hanson and one of his officers were soon there. Hanson concurred with Davis's conclusion that someone had searched the house looking for something. "It's interesting that Devan's room, and the room of his best friend Max, and now Janie's house have all been searched by someone. Do you think Rhodes was killed because someone wanted something he had, but not finding it, is now searching for it among those closest to him?" Davis asked Chief Hanson.

"That would certainly seem to be a possibility." The police chief nodded his head in agreement.

"Is there someone you can call to come and stay with you tonight?" Davis asked Janie and her mother before he left. "I hate to leave you here alone."

"We'll be all right," Janie assured him. "I'll keep the doors locked, and if we hear or see anything, we'll call the police. They're less than five minutes away."

"Call me if I'm needed," Davis told the young clerk.

"You know I will. I didn't hesitate to call you this afternoon, did I?" Janie smiled at her friend before giving him a hug.

As Davis was going down the porch steps toward his Jeep he spotted someone in the window across the street watching him. *I believe that is Mrs. Lane*, Davis concluded knowing that the widow, now well up in years, lived in the house across the street. *Maybe she saw something*, he speculated. Instead of going to his Jeep in the driveway, Davis continued to walk across the street. He saw the figure in the window disappear when it was obvious he was coming her way.

Davis rang the doorbell, but wasn't sure if it was in working order, so he knocked a couple of times and waited. An elderly lady leaning on a walker was soon at the door. "Mrs. Lane, I'm Davis Morgan. Perhaps you remember me visiting with you in the hospital several months ago when I was the interim preacher at the church."

"Yes, I remember you when you were just a boy. You used to mow some lawns on the street."

Davis had almost forgotten that when he was in his early teens, he kept up the lawns of several people, three or four on this street, for three to five dollars each and, at that time, thought he was in high cotton. "You're right, Mrs. Lane. That's been a while."

"It doesn't seem like very long ago to an old lady like me. Time passes quickly."

"I know what you're talking about. That's starting to happen to me too." Davis smiled at the lady in the doorway. "Rita and Janie had a prowler a little while ago while they were out. I was wondering if maybe you saw anything that might help us find the culprit." Not wanting to alarm the elderly lady who lived alone

Davis tried to be careful about how he stated his questions. "Did you see anyone over there while they were gone?"

"As a matter of fact, I did." Mrs. Lane was now speaking louder than before. "You understand that I don't sit at the window and spy on the neighbors, but shortly after they left, I saw a black car pull into the driveway. I couldn't make out the numbers or letters on the license plate, but I could tell it wasn't a Georgia plate. A young man with long curly red hair got out of the car and went to the door. It looked like he fiddled with the door for a minute and then opened it to go inside the house. I had never seen him over there before, but I decided he must be a relative or maybe one of Janie's friends since he evidently had a key."

"How long did he stay?" Davis asked.

"I didn't pay much attention," she answered. "But it had to be about twenty-seven or twenty-eight minutes since Gilligan's Island was coming on when he got there and was going off when he left."

"You've been very helpful," Davis told Mrs. Lane. "Chief Hanson and one of his officers are investigating. I'm going to tell him about what you saw, and he will probably want to talk with you about it."

"I would be glad to talk with him." She responded, recognizing that she played an important role in this whole adventure. "If you are still mowing lawns, I could use a good worker to take care of mine." Mrs. Lane spoke with a little grin on her face as he was leaving.

"I've not done that for a while, but if my business doesn't pick up soon, I may take you up on your offer." Davis walked back over to Janie's house to inform the chief about the witness before he got into his Jeep to drive home.

Deidre had not yet arrived home when Davis got to the house. There was no reason for him to start dinner since this was their regular night to eat at Cracker Barrel. Davis picked up his Bible, which he had neglected in the last few days. One of his reoccurring themes while in the ministry was, Read the Word. Of course, he felt like a hypocrite when he himself did not do that. Davis turned to the beginning of his favorite book in the Bible—the Book of Psalms. He read the very first chapter which he had long ago committed to memory from the King James Version, but he was now reading from the New International Version.

Verse 3 caught Davis's attention. Speaking of the one who puts his trust in the Lord it says, *He is like a tree planted by streams of water, which yields its fruit in season and whose leaf does not wither. Whatever he does prospers.*

Davis thought about the big white oak tree out at Spring Bank where he and Janie had found Devan's body. That tree stood near a small creek fed by a nearby spring. It had stood strong and healthy with its roots deep for maybe three hundred years. That was Davis's goal in life, to stand with healthy roots deep in the Lord right on into eternity. The last phase in that verse used to confuse Davis. Was it saying that such a person will always be prosperous in matters the world sees as wealth? Davis had come to understand that the psalmist was speaking of something different. He was talking of a life that remained useful on into eternity. That was Davis's goal for his own life, to be useful to God and the people around him.

Davis's mind went to his special young friend, Charley. He wanted so much for Charley to find the blessings he himself had found in the Lord. Over the past couple of years Charley had become the closest thing he had to a brother. The condition in which he found Charley today was an indication of a giant setback, and it troubled him deeply. He knew he would have to regroup, but he would not be discouraged in his efforts on Charley's behalf. He would be more diligent than before, and he was sure the day of victory would come.

Davis lowered his head and shut his eyes to silently pray for Charley. Caught up in his time with the Father, Davis did not hear

Deidre enter the room. "I caught you napping." She remarked when he opened his eyes and looked up at her."

"I don't guess you'd believe I was praying?" he asked her with a smile.

"Knowing your reliance on prayer, I would have no trouble at all believing that." Deidre told him before walking over to the chair where he sat and leaning over to kiss him.

Within ten minutes, they were on their way to the restaurant. They remained there well over an hour, not the result of slow service, but rather the time it takes for two people deeply devoted to one another to share the day they had spent apart. Considering the last couple of days, Davis wondered what tomorrow would bring. It had to be better, he decided. *Or did it? Sometimes when things start to roll downhill they just keep rolling.*

CHAPTER 6

One Thursday morning out of each month Deidre was required to be at school early to meet with the student history club. Today was that Thursday, and Davis decided it would be a good day for him to have breakfast with the guys at the Little Rock Café. These were fellows in Davis's age bracket that he had known for most of his life. They ate breakfast at the Little Rock Café Monday through Friday of every week. Davis was often part of the group in the first months after he returned to Adairsville, in the days before he and Deidre were married. When he had the opportunity, he still liked to occasionally drop-by for breakfast and a time of playful, verbal jousting with the fellas.

When Davis arrived at the little diner, the dining room was buzzing and pretty much full, but for the two tables in the northwest corner where only one gentleman was seated. Davis immediately recognized him as Red Edwards, owner of the Adairsville Hardware. "Everyone else running late this morning?" Davis asked while sitting himself in a chair beside his longtime friend.

"It's getting toward the end of the week. The guys get run-down and become a little slower," the man with the sandy red hair told him.

"But not you," Davis replied. "You're still going strong."

"That's right, the years have taken less of a toll on me than the others." Red laughed before coming clean. "The fact is, I probably do a whole lot less physical labor than most of the other guys. I've probably got a little more left than most of them, but if you tell them I said that, I'll deny it down to my last breath."

After a couple of minutes Dean Nelson, Charley's brother and the owner of Nelson's Auto repair, came into the room with Brad Dewelt, the Adairsville fire chief. Dean, unlike his brother, a big man approaching three hundred pounds, had thirty years earlier made a major splash as a two-way lineman on the Tigers football team. Many people in the know felt he could have participated well in Division I football and perhaps in the pros. But that was not to be. Dean didn't do well with the books, and his love for Sherrie kept calling him home. Dean was home, married and starting his auto repair business before his football career got started.

"Well, we are honored today. It looks like *The Preacher* is in the house," Brad said looking toward Davis and extending his right hand. "I suppose we'll have to behave ourselves."

"His presence never made much difference in our behavior before," Dean declared. All three of the good-natured guys who delighted in trying to make Davis's life miserable laughed. A few moments later, Al Jensen, the banker in the group, and Bobby Thorton, who recently moved his real estate business to Adairsville, came in to find seats at the table. Bobby was the quarterback on the same high school teams on which Davis and Dean played but had moved to west central Georgia for years before recently returning to his home town.

Brenda, the waitress who could not only handle the group's razzing well but delighted in throwing it right back, appeared at the table to take their orders. "Is this everyone today? It seems you guys are starting to have a lot of dropouts. People starting to be concerned about their reputations I suppose."

"No, it's not that," Brad countered. "We're such an exclusive club that most men have a hard time maintaining the qualifications. That's why the preacher here only occasionally shows up. When he starts to rise to our standards, we'll probably let him spend more time with us."

"That's a laugh," Brenda briskly responded. "It's probably his friendship with you bums that keeps you out of jail."

"Always good to have some ties to law enforcement," Bobby spoke up. "You're still the chaplain of our rag tag crime squad aren't you, Davis?"

"Hey, watch how you speak of our boys in blue," Dean snapped back. "My little brother is a big part of that force."

"I know he is." Bobbly quickly replied not wanting to offend his long-time friend. "Not only is he part of the department, but I think there is no finer officer than Charley. He's a lot like Chief, isn't he?" Bobby referred to Dean and Charley's father who patrolled the streets of Adairsville alone in his own car for many years.

"Too bad Dean didn't turn out more like his dad," Al suggested. "Then we could have two Nelsons watching over our town." Al obviously knew that such a statement always got a rise out of Dean.

"Not me," Dean answered. "Charley's life is police work and mine is engines. I live in hope that someday my little brother will come to his senses and accept my invitation to be my partner. He's an exceptional mechanic, you know."

"Talking about the police, I hear they have a new murder case on their hands. Have you guys heard that one of the big wig movie guys was found shot. Know anything about that Preacher?" Al asked Davis.

The fact that Davis was hearing no phases like body magnet was evidence that word had not yet leaked that he found the body. He was greatly relieved and didn't volunteer that information. He knew he would pay for it later when they learned of his involvement. "No, our boys will have little to do with that investigation. The body was found down near Kingston. That's in the jurisdiction of the sheriff's department," Davis told them.

"I hear the victim was Janie's boyfriend." Brad said. "If that's true, I wouldn't be surprised if Old Lady Edison is the culprit.

My cousin, Bruce, dated Janie for a while, but I think the old lady caused him to lose interest. He said she was enormously possessive of Janie's time and was really hostile at times. Bruce said she had an old gun, and he didn't think she would hesitate to use it."

Brenda returned with their orders and distributed the appropriate dishes to their proper places before walking away. "You guys let me know if you need anything, but remember, I'm not exclusively your waitress. I've got other customers to wait on," she facetiously told them.

"Incidentally," Red spoke up, "Have you fellows heard what's happening with Tommy Black?"

Davis was relieved that the conversation moved away from the murder of Devan Rhodes.

"He's tearing up the Carolina League at Salem," Red announced. "Hitting well over three hundred with six or seven homers and playing a great third base. I bet he's less than two years away from Fenway Park."

"I thought we'd lost that boy and all his potential," Al added. "I think we owe the preacher for that one."

"All I did was make a Red Sox scout I knew back in my Indianapolis days aware of Tommy's talents. The rest took care of itself," Davis told the men.

"Oh, it was more than that," Dean replied. "I happen to know for a fact that you gave some time to getting that boy back on the right track."

"I spent a little time with him, but Tommy's basically a good kid who simply needed a little nudge." Davis, extremely proud of the young athlete, was reluctant to share more of the story with his friends.

Davis heard a voice he recognized coming from behind him. "Some of our most distinguished citizens all gathered over here in the corner," Mayor Sam Ellison belted out in his booming voice causing most of the other people in the restaurant to turn and look his way. He then proceeded to shake the hand of each man.

"I need to talk with you, Davis. I would like for you to work with us on a committee," Sam said when he took Davis's right hand.

"No, thank you, Mr. Mayor. I'm not taking on any new responsibility since I discovered I have a heart problem."

"Do we have anymore movie companies scheduled to come to town, Sam?" Red asked the mayor. "This one has been a big plus for us out at the hardware store and lumber yard. I had no idea it took so much lumber to build props for a movie set."

"We're working on it! You can be sure we are doing everything possible to grow our little town. Things are hopping. Who knows what tomorrow will bring." The Mayor declared before walking over to a table to confer with a couple of other constituents.

"I didn't know it was election time," Bobby stated after the mayor left their table.

"It's nowhere near election day. He's that way all the time," Dean surmised.

"Don't forget the tips." Banker Al Jensen spoke loudly when after a few minutes, they began to push their chairs back to scatter to their various responsibilities. "Brenda works hard and has two children to support. Be generous!"

"I need to talk with you, Dean." Davis told the big guy when they reached the parking lot.

"Yea, I thought you might. You saw Charley yesterday, didn't you?"

"Yes, I did, and I was really upset at the condition in which I found him."

"I guess you know the story behind the story. He's losing his girl, you know. Charley has done his share of drinking in the past, but nothing serious. I don't remember him ever tying one on like that."

"He's pretty well stayed away from the sauce for at least the last six months," Davis stated. "But I know this thing with Tonya hit him hard. I think it would be good for both of us to stick sort of close to him over the next few weeks."

"That's probably true, but it won't be easy. Charley has always been so horribly independent. When he was a little kid, he always had to do things his way, and he spent half his time wandering around in the woods by himself with that old twenty-two he had." Dean told his longtime friend.

"I think he's passed that now and has come to realize that he doesn't want to live his life alone. I think that's why Tonya's moving hit him so hard. It seems to me he had concluded that Tonya was the one with whom he wanted to spend his life. Well, I don't want to keep you," Davis said. "I just wanted to make sure you knew what was going on. I don't know about you, but I've got some work to do."

"You don't know what work is," Dean responded with a grin. "Come by the garage sometime, and I'll give you a demonstration of real work."

CHAPTER 7

Davis parked his Jeep down by the railroad. He hoped the spaces closer to the 1902 Stock Exchange would be needed for potential customers. He could surely use the business. Pam was still substituting for Janie and smiled when he came through the door. "Morning," she said.

"Good morning Miss Pam. Looks like it's going to be a beautiful Adairsville day," Davis responded energetically.

"Maybe a little warmer than I like it this time of year, but I guess I shouldn't complain." Her voice dropped with the last statement, but then rose when she continued. "My family and I are looking for a church home. I understand your church has a new preacher. Can you tell me anything about him?"

"I'm just getting to know him, but I've been impressed with what I've learned so far. I've heard him preach four times, and I can honestly tell you that his sermons have been exceptional. He genuinely seems to care about people and is certainly a friendly sort. I think he's just a good ole South Carolina boy."

"Is that where he's from, South Carolina?"

"Born and bred, I think," Davis answered. "Most recently he lived in Spartanburg. One of our men heard him speak while visiting relatives in that city, was impressed, and that started the ball rolling. Why don't you come and visit us this Lord's Day? Deidre and I would be happy to meet you and your family in front of the church and have you sit with us during the service."

"We will be out of town this coming Sunday," Pam hastily replied, "But I'm going to take you up on that offer soon."

Always hard to break the ice and come that first time. Davis's mind still worked a little like the pastor he was for almost half his life. *But I'm not going to ignore the open door. A simple invitation is rarely enough. The barriers must be removed to get a person in a church the first time. It sure would be great to have Pam and her family as a part of our church family.*

Davis did his usual morning cleanup in the shop and spent some time pricing new stock he recently purchased. *Seems like I'm buying a lot more than I'm selling,* he thought. *If I'm going to make a go of this, I've got to do a better job of practicing some sound business principles.* Davis knew that one of the secrets to a successful bookstore was always having fresh stock to attract the booklovers who were his regulars, but he also was aware that one could never make any money by always investing more than he sold.

Davis was in the tearoom with a newspaper in hand, finishing up the chicken salad sandwich he ordered for lunch, when he heard Charley's voice behind him. "Davis, I guess I owe you an apology."

"Why do you think you owe me an apology?" Davis turned to look at the young officer in uniform who still appeared less than one hundred percent.

"I didn't like the condition in which you found me yesterday. What you saw was not the real me, and I'm sorry you saw me that way."

"Are you sorry I saw you or remorseful about getting that way in the first place?"

There was a moment of silence before Charley spoke. "I think I'm embarrassed on both counts. I'm sorry I didn't show more restraint, and I'm sorry you saw me."

"Then we need to just forget the whole affair. We don't have to speak of it again."

"I appreciate your attitude and your friendship, Davis, but before we leave the subject, I've got a question. I'm not looking for one of your sermons, but I need to ask, in your estimation, is it wrong to take a drink now and then? We don't talk about it, but I think you know that, primarily due to your influence, over the past year or two, I'm trying to grow up and live a little better than I did in the past. Despite what you saw yesterday, ordinarily, I'm not a drunk, but I've been known to take a drink or two in the past, mostly in social settings or just to unwind when I get home from a hard day of duty. Is that wrong?"

A couple came into the tearoom and was seated only two tables away. "Let's go back to the shop where we can have a little privacy," Davis suggested quietly. The two men walked to the back where Davis located two rather uncomfortable folding chairs and arranged them with one facing the other. He sat down in one and motioned for Charley to take the other.

"Charley, you asked if it is *wrong* to now and then take a drink. There is only one source for knowing right and wrong and that is the Bible. So, without going into one of my sermons, as you say, let me share two verses from the Bible."

"That's okay, but remember, I'm on duty and can't stay here all afternoon," Charley responded.

"I understand, and I promise I'll not take more than five minutes."

"Then go for it," Charley suggested.

Davis reached behind himself to take his Bible from a small table. "In 1 Timothy 5:23 The Apostles Paul tells the young preacher, Timothy, '*Stop drinking only water, and use a little wine because of your stomach and your frequent illnesses.*'"

"So, it's all right to drink using some restraint?" Charley asked.

"I don't think that's what is being said. It's true that a lot of people quote that verse to justify their drinking, at least in moderation, but all Paul is saying there is, it's valid in some cases to use alcohol for medicinal purposes. For example, when you have a bad cough and the doctor prescribes a cough medicine that is thirty percent alcohol. But let's look at another verse. Davis turned in his Bible to Ephesians 5:18 and read just loud enough for Charley to hear, *"Do not get drunk on wine, which leads to debauchery. Instead, be filled with the Spirit."*

"My honesty compels me to say that, while the writer is instructing us not to become drunk or intoxicated, he doesn't rule out an occasional nip, nor do I find any passage that does so, but is it always wise to do what we are not forbidden to do? Sometimes it is wise to abstain even from the unforbidden. Look at verse 15 in chapter 5 from which I just read. *Be very careful, then, how you live—not as unwise but as wise.* Charley, I've always been a teetotaler, and that is my plan for the rest of my life because it's the wise thing to do."

Davis observed two people, a man and a woman, come into the shop to browse. "I'll be with you in a moment," he called out to them.

"Why do you say it is wise to abstain altogether?" Charley asked.

"Let me quickly give you the short version. Some people have a chemical intolerance to alcohol. Simply stated, they can't handle it. Others over time may become more and more dependent on it to the extent that it starts to destroy their lives. And even if that is not the case, there are those we influence, such as our children, who may be influenced to follow our example, and they may not be able to handle it. As a minister, I counseled countless people whose lives and marriages were total mayhem because of alcohol. I'm sure as a police officer, you have seen the same. My opinion, then, is that we're being foolish when we even dabble with something that has such potential for our destruction, and even worse, the ruin of people we love. So, wisdom compels me to be a teetotaler. If you want to talk about it more, we can sit down sometime in the future."

"What you said makes a lot of sense. I'm going to give it some thought," Charley told him. "There are a couple of other things I need to tell you before I go."

"That's fine, but first let me see if I can assist these folks," Davis said.

"Can I help you?" Davis asked when he approached his potential customers.

"We're just browsing. You have an extraordinary selection," the gentleman told Davis.

"Thank you, sir," Davis responded. "Let me know if I can help you find a book or a section. I'll be over there." Davis pointed toward where Charley was seated before strolling back in that direction.

When Davis was again seated in the chair he had occupied earlier, Charley, aware that others were in the shop, spoke in a quiet tone. "I did some checking on Devan Rhodes and found he was pretty much a law-abiding citizen. But I did find a couple of interesting facts. The first is that he was involved with his sister in a dispute over the family fortune. It seems his mother became disillusioned about him at some point shortly before her death and changed her will, eliminating him and leaving everything to his sister, Jeanette Odon. The change in the will was a quick, informal process that was never put in the hands of an attorney. The sister had possession of it until a few weeks ago when it came up missing. She accused Devan of stealing it. The dispute, it seems, has swelled to a full-blown family war."

"That fits," Davis declared with some enthusiasm. "That could be what the guy with the red hair is looking for, and it could be what caused Devan to lose his life."

"Possibly," Charley cautiously declared. "The second thing goes way back, fifteen years ago when Devan was in his late teens, and it probably has nothing to do with what happened here. He was a witness to a murder in Elbert County that has never been solved."

"Elbert County, Georgia?" Davis asked, looking a little confused. "I didn't think Devan ever lived in Georgia."

"He didn't," Charley answered. "At the time he lived in Anderson, South Carolina, which is only about thirty-six miles from Elberton, Georgia." Charley continued to tell the story while looking down at notes he made earlier. "He was with a group of guys who had gone to a small track in nearby Commerce, Georgia, earlier that day. The young man, who turned out to be the victim, had participated in the race and was driving a pick-up and towing his race car. Devan was in the seat beside him. The other three boys were in a car following when a blue mustang passed them. A passenger in the mustang threw a bottle at the truck hitting the driver's side window and then sped ahead. They caught the mustang and the two vehicles were used to block him in. The driver of the pickup got out with a wooden baseball bat, walked to the trapped mustang and used the bat to break the windshield. They got back into their vehicles and the mustang took off down the road before turning around. While driving past the young man who had used the bat, the driver fired several rounds from a pistol at the mustang, killing the race car driver. Devan, who had a good view from the front seat, always contended he would know the shooter if he ever saw him again."

"Fifteen years ago, and never solved. I can't imagine what that could have to do with his death here in Adairsville," Davis surmised.

"I agree, but I've learned to leave no stone unturned," Charley replied. The two friends walked toward the front door. "Incidentally, have you talked with Tonya yet?"

"We're going out for a late dinner this evening." Charley grinned.

"Davis, could you please come to the front." Pam's voice seemed slightly stressed. "There's someone up here who would like to talk with you."

Davis wondered, as he started toward the checkout counter what this was about. Usually when someone wanted to see him, they were sent back to his corner rather than his being summoned to the front. When they reached Pam's spot in the store, they spotted a beautiful tall young lady fully decked out in what had to be a designer outfit that looked lovely on the blonde. Davis saw Charley do a double take. He estimated her to be in her late twenties or early thirties. "This is Caroline Roberson," Pam announced to them. "Devan Rhodes's fiancée."

CHAPTER 8

L etting that last statement sink in, there was at first only silence from the two men. Finally, Davis spoke up, "Ms. Robertson, I'm Davis Morgan and this is Charley Nelson. If we look a little surprised, it's because we didn't know Devan had a fiancée."

"I can believe that. I recently discovered that Devan didn't often advertise that fact, but the truth is, we've been officially engaged now for more than five months. See," Caroline said, holding her left hand up to reveal a rather impressive diamond on her ring finger.

"Let me express my sympathy for your loss," Davis reacted to the news. "What can I do for you?"

"I understand you and a young lady who works in this establishment discovered Devan's body. I want to learn as much as I can about what happened and wondered what you can tell me."

"Yes, Janie and I found Devan. I don't want to sound insensitive, but all that I can tell you is that we found him, apparently shot in the chest, lying under a big oak tree. He was already deceased when we arrived."

"And who is this Janie person of whom you speak?" the young woman asked.

"As you mentioned a moment ago, she works here at the 1902 Stock Exchange. I don't know how to tell you this, but uh..." Davis stuttered.

"You don't have to be considerate of my feelings, Mr. Morgan. I knew Devan well, and I know he sometimes saw other women."

"It's true, he and Janie had dated almost since the time he came to Adairsville, but I can assure you Janie had no idea he was seriously involved with anyone else," Davis said.

"Maybe she didn't want to know," Ms. Robertson responded.

"No, I don't believe that. Janie isn't that kind of girl. She wouldn't have consented to date Devan if she'd known he was seriously committed to someone else."

"If you look closely, Mr. Morgan, I think you'll find that just about every girl is that kind of girl," Devan's fiancée shot back.

"That's a rather cynical view, Ms. Robertson. But the fact is, I know a lot of ladies who are not those kinds of girls. Here in Adairsville, we call it *morality*." Davis spoke while directing a smile toward the physically lovely young woman who showed little evidence of possessing a matching *inner* beauty.

"You're the one who's naïve, Morgan." The girl raised her voice in an unfriendly manner when she spoke.

"I certainly don't want to offend you, Ms. Robertson. I know this has got to be a bad time for you." Davis attempted to turn the conversation in a more pleasant direction.

Charley, who had remained perfectly silent up to this point, jumped in. "Where are you from Ms. Robertson?" He bluntly asked.

"I live in LA," she hesitantly answered.

"Down here, that can be either Los Angeles, California, or Lower Alabama," Charley responded with a chuckle.

"I'm from Los Angeles, California." Caroline replied not smiling, obviously not appreciating Charley's little joke. "I'm an actress, and I write romantic novels," she said rather proudly.

"I was wondering when you got to town, Ms. Robertson. When did you arrive?" Charley asked.

"I arrived in Atlanta five days ago. I had some business there, but I didn't get to this hole you people call a town until yesterday." The young woman from LA turned toward the doorway now seemingly anxious to escape Charley's interrogation. "If you have more questions for me, you'll have to contact my lawyers." She directed her words to Charley as she briskly left the building, her high heels rapidly tapping on the concrete floor.

Pam, who had stood silent through the entire ordeal, now had her mouth open and a confused look on her face. "Okay, back to work now," she said, evidently at a loss for words. She started to fiddle with some papers on the check-out counter.

Davis walked with Charley out to his patrol car. "What do you think? Is it possible we have another suspect?" Charley asked.

"That would certainly appear to be the case," Davis answered. "How often does the jilted lover turn out to be the guilty party?"

"It happens," Charley nonchalantly replied. "But in this case, it would seem to me that Janie would have been the likely victim."

"You might be right. Our gorgeous actress/romance writer from LA seems to be a rather cold fish," Davis remarked.

***

The slim red-headed man with the long hair and bushy sideburns left his motel room and got into his ancient black Cadillac. It's *old*, he told himself, *but it's a gem, still gets me anywhere I want to go in style*. Noticing two ladies in the parking lot staring at him, he decided he would soon find a barber shop to get a serious haircut and a clean shave. He was becoming more and more aware that his look was attracting a lot of attention in the conservative confines of Adairsville, Georgia, and if there was anything he didn't want to do, it was to draw attention to himself.

The red-headed man continued to drive south on Interstate 75 toward Cartersville. He wanted to find a good restaurant where he could get a suitable meal with the proper drink. He continued to observe in his rear-view mirror a tan Ford several car lengths behind him, but he thought little of it since he was driving slightly over the speed limit and figured the driver was using him as a buffer. He, himself, often did that when traveling on freeways.

Let the jerks issue citations to the guy ahead of me, I don't need to be using my hard-earned money to support the man.

Still not familiar with the area, the red-headed man took the first Cartersville exit. He was annoyed to find himself on a country road and upon glancing in the mirror, saw the tan car was still behind him. He wondered... Then suddenly the driver stomped the accelerator and streaked to a position beside him in the lane for oncoming traffic. When the driver pulled even with him, the red-headed man saw that the window on the passenger side was down, and the driver had on what looked like an old Richard Nixon Halloween mask. Then the driver lifted his right hand to clearly reveal a pistol. There was no doubt about what *Mr. Nixon* had in mind!

The red-headed man slammed on his brakes just as he heard the gun shot. The sound of the shot told him that metal had been hit. There now had to be a severe hole or dent somewhere on his beloved Caddy. That didn't concern him as much as what was happening up ahead. He saw the tan car skid into a turn and start back toward him. There was not time for him to turn around his own vehicle to speed away from his pursuer. Instead he hit the accelerator racing toward the car with as much speed as he could muster. It would be a game of "chicken," he decided as he headed straight toward the Ford. The red-headed man could see the driver now holding his gun in his left hand since he, no doubt, was right handed and needed his best hand to control his car. The masked man swerved as they met and never got off a shot.

The red-headed man watched in his rearview mirror to see the tan car disappear. Only then did he let out a sigh of relief. *And I thought this was going to be a simple job with no danger attached. Shows you what I know.* He sat for a moment before finally driving ahead to see if he could find the way to Cartersville. He still needed to eat, and boy did he need a drink.

***

Charley and Tonya had their late dinner at the Adairsville Inn. At the table, they chatted and occasionally giggled without saying anything about their last date or the news Tonya divulged on that occasion. After the young couple left the dining room, the doors were locked to customers, but there were still lights and noises on the inside as the workers cleaned-up. "Let's sit and talk for a while," Charley suggested. He took Tonya's hand and led her to a bench under a large oak tree in a small garden behind the restaurant building.

"I suppose I will be safe out here since there's a policeman present and a mighty good one at that." Tonya smiled at her date before being seated.

"I'm sorry for the way I acted the other night," Charley looked down at the ground as he spoke. "I had no right to say the things I said," he uttered, now gazing directly into those beautiful brown eyes. "I acted like a jerk."

"No, you didn't. I threw it at you all at once. I should've discussed it with you, and together we could've come to a decision. I have as much reason to apologize to you as you do to me."

"When will you be leaving?" Charley asked.

"I'll drive down with my U-Haul trailer two weeks from the day after tomorrow."

"I'll see if the chief will schedule that weekend off for me, and I'll help do the driving," Charley told her.

"You don't have to do that. I can handle it."

"There's no doubt in my mind that you can handle it. You can handle anything you decide to do. I'm absolutely convinced of that, and that's just one of the many reasons I love you." Charley squeezed her hand. "I want to make the trip for me, not because you need the help. I need to see where you'll be living, and I guess I want to feel like I'm a part of the venture."

"You're a rare one, Charley." Tonya leaned over to gently kiss him. They sat for a couple of minutes with no words at all before Charley spoke again.

"What about your house? What arrangements have you made for it?" he inquired.

"I've found a renter, a widow lady from Cass named Mrs. Wayble. I think it'll be a good arrangement. She can pay the small rent payment which I'm going to need, and she has a son in the area who can help her with minor maintenance."

"Sounds like you've got all the bases covered," Charley acknowledged.

"All but one," Tonya responded.

"And what is that?" Charley inquired.

"I haven't figured out how I'm going to get along down there in Jacksonville without having you close by. I don't think I had any idea how much I loved you until I found myself facing being separated from you."

"We'll make sure we're together as much as possible," Charley told her. "Someone reminded me the other day that Jacksonville isn't that far away, and after all I'm a pilot—admittedly, a pilot without a plane, but rentals aren't hard to get."

"You'd better be careful. Too many of those rentals could make a poor man of you," Tonya answered.

"It'll be worth it to be with you." Charley told her before embracing her for a serious kiss, which she returned.

"What's going on here?" Charley recognized the voice of the uniformed man holding the flashlight. It was Jed, his sometimes partner, and his companion when both had been wounded six months earlier in the storage bin caper.

"Can't anyone get any privacy around here," Charley protested.

"You know it's my job to keep this sort of thing down around here. You two kids better go on home before I call your parents." The young policeman laughed.

CHAPTER 9

"I'm so glad it's not raining today like it has the last two Saturdays. I've been looking forward to this trip," Deidre informed her husband who was sitting in the rocking chair beside her wicker seat on their front porch.

"Sometime soon, we'll take a real trip," Davis responded. "I know you need to get away."

"We can plan to do that after Amy and Jay's baby comes. Driving to Ellijay is a treat for me now. You know how much I enjoy the antique stores," Deidre reminded him.

"Maybe today you'll find that Tiffany-style lamp you've been looking for so long."

"I just hope, if it does show up in one of the stores, we'll be able to afford it. They can be awfully expensive."

"We'll see," Davis responded with a smile. "I can all ways sell my Jeep to get the money."

"That'll be the day!" Deidre retorted. "I'm thinking you would sell me before you'd part with the Jeep."

"Now, you know better than that. I wouldn't exchange you for anything in this world," Davis assured her.

"Not even a first edition of *To Kill a Mockingbird?*"

"Now that you mention it, I would have to think seriously about that," he joked.

Deidre gave him a repulsed look, and then broke into a smile when her husband said, "no, not even a perfect copy with a perfect dust jacket. You're far more valuable than that," he assured her and leaned over to kiss her.

"You'd better be careful. What'll the neighbors say?" she asked.

"They'll say, 'there's a man who loves his wife,'" Davis remarked.

"And a wife who loves her husband," Deidre countered before kissing his cheek.

"Where are Jay and Amy? They were supposed to be here by a quarter till ten and it's already well past the hour," Davis pointed out, looking at the time on his phone.

"You have to allow for Amy's condition," Deidre suggested. "She's not moving at the same rate of speed these days as in the past."

"I suppose you're right. I'm going to have to be a little more patient, I guess."

Less than ten minutes later Jay and Amy pulled into the driveway. Davis and Deidre rose from their seats and hurried to Jay's car where they climbed into the back seat. "Ready for an excursion to the mountains?" Jay questioned his passengers. "We would've been here earlier, but we overslept and then I had to feed the horses before eating breakfast and showering."

"He's lying to you," Amy told them. "He got all that done and then still had to wait on me for half an hour."

"None of that matters," Deidre said. "We're on our way, and we're going to have a great time."

Jay backed the car out of the driveway and pointed it toward their destination. It felt a little odd for Davis to be in the back seat, but he appreciated Jay agreeing to drive. His full-sized Chevy was much more comfortable for four people than the Jeep. As they passed the Burger King, an older black Cadillac was ready to enter the highway at the traffic light to their left. Davis, remembering the description of the car driven by the man with the long red hair turned his head to try to get a good look at the driver. *That could be him.* Davis, not getting a good look turned almost all the way around when Jay drove past the interchange.

"What're you looking at?" Deidre asked. "See somebody you know?"

"No, I don't think so. You know how curious I am."

That was probably him, and if it was, I bet he's staying in the hotel on the hill. With Deidre and Amy in the car, I can't ask Jay to turn around and follow him. I would never get out of the doghouse. I'll have to check it out when we return.

It usually took them about an hour to get to Ellijay, but to-day it took a little longer because they stopped at the Panorama Apple House where both couples left with bags of apples, but more importantly, they each purchased a fried apple pie. All four were munching on the treat before they got back to the car. "To fully enjoy them, you've got to eat them while they're still hot," Deidre explained.

"Amy has been talking about those pies all week," Jay told them.

"I'm thinking we may have to stop again on our way home," Amy, who had already devoured her pie, suggested.

"I'm thinking, at this point, you might need to limit the fried food," Jay only half-jokingly told his wife.

"I know," she responded obviously disappointed. "But they're so good."

Jay found a parking spot in downtown Ellijay, and they walked a couple of blocks to one of the antique malls where they spent over an hour examining the merchandise. It was in the booths with books where Davis could most often be found. Even though there were books for sale throughout the large building, Davis soon learned that those that were desirable were priced too high to buy for resale.

The ladies sort of went their own way. Deidre and Amy were not your typical stepmother and daughter. Their ages were only about five years apart, and they had been best friends for much longer than Davis and Deidre had been married. They seemed to have a good time. The men were delighted to see their wives enjoying themselves. After leaving the antique mall without buying even one item, the small group of sightseers walked down the street toward the middle of town. "Isn't it just about lunch time?" Jay asked.

"I was thinking that myself," Davis agreed.

"You guys are only interested in the food. Let's stop at a couple of the smaller shops." Amy was already moving toward the door of one that looked interesting. The guys endured two more such stores before finding themselves at Cantaberry Restaurant, a quaint little establishment that specializes in soups and sandwiches. Each ordered a half-sandwich. Deidre and Amy both had heard the tomato basil soup was the house special, so they had that while the guys both ordered chili.

"You know there are two more good-sized antique malls just a block or two away. Are you up for checking those out?" Davis asked his daughter.

"We're here. Might as well take it all in. Besides, Deidre hasn't found her lamp yet. I can handle it."

"You let us know if you get tired. I can go get the car and bring it to you," her husband told her.

Davis was tempted by the coconut cake but having started the outing with dessert, they all passed.

After spending over two more hours in antique shops, they were ready to start home without Deidre finding her lamp. Davis observed that Amy, despite her condition, seemed to be less exhausted than the rest of them. *That's my Amy,* Davis thought. *Few people live more energetically than her.*

Deidre catnapped on the way home while Davis could only think about questioning a hotel clerk about a red-headed man and a black Caddy.

***

"I need to go to the Food Lion to pick up a few things. Do you want to go with me?" Deidre asked Davis shortly after Jay and Amy dropped them off at home.

"I've a couple of errands to run. I think I'll take care of those while you're shopping. Then we can settle in for a quiet evening."

"Sounds good to me, I should return in less than an hour," Deidre told him.

Less than three minutes after Deidre drove out of the driveway, Davis was in his Jeep on the way to the hotel. *If I hurry, I can be back before she returns, and she'll be none the wiser to what I've been up to.* Davis felt bad about deceiving Deidre but rationalized that his deception was for her own good. He didn't want her worrying about him.

Arriving at the Magnuson Hotel, Davis was pleased to see the clerk on duty was Jenny Lawson, a friend, close to his own age that he'd known for most of his life. They played together as children.

"Jenny, good to see you. It's been awhile. You're looking younger than when we were back in high school. How's that handsome husband getting along?" Davis spoke with a rapid delivery and a big smile.

"What're you up to, Davis Morgan? I know you well enough to read you like a book. What do you want from me?"

She's the one who ought to be the detective, Davis decided. "Never could pull anything over on you, Jenny. I've got just a couple of simple questions."

"I won't guarantee any answers, but you go ahead and ask your questions."

Davis could see Jenny bracing herself as she prepared to hear what he had on his mind. *This may not be so easy,* Davis thought. "This morning I saw a gentleman with long red hair, driving an older model black Cadillac, turning into the road down at the bottom of the hill. Can you tell me if he is staying here, and if so, give me any information you have about him?"

"You don't want much, do you?" Jenny answered, obviously annoyed at his questions. "All you want is to get me fired. You know I can't give you that kind of information. I need this job to help put food on the table," She obviously was stretching the truth since Davis knew, for a fact, she and Steve were not destitute.

"Jenny, you know I'm chaplain with the police department, and this is kind of official business."

"I know that being the chaplain gives you no official status at all. Besides that, I couldn't even give those answers to the chief without a warrant."

"But Jenny this..."

"Don't 'but Jenny' me. There's nothing you can say that'll change my mind. If I could, Davis, I would help you. You've always been a good friend, but I can't. I need this job."

"Okay, Jenny, I understand. I'll just have to come up with another way to get my information. Thanks, anyway." Davis muttered as he turned toward the door. Davis wondered how Charley always managed to get answers even from people he didn't know, while it never seemed to work for him. Was it the uniform, or was it Charley's charm?

"No hard feelings," Jenny called out to him as he was leaving the room, walking toward the parking lot.

"No hard feelings," he shouted back. "Have a good evening."

At that moment Davis raised his head to look up, finding himself almost bumping into a slim gentleman perhaps an inch or two taller than himself. He casually stared into the face of the oncoming man who intensely glared back at him. He had long red hair, bushy sideburns, and a mustache that turned downward. Davis tensed up and almost stopped in his tracks. *That's him, that's the cowardly Lion!* Davis glanced ahead to see a black Cadillac in a parking space just ahead of him. He experienced a moment of blank panic. What should he do?

CHAPTER 10

When the panic ended, Davis suddenly realized he didn't have to do anything. This man didn't know him, nor had he ever seen him. He nodded at the red-headed man and spoke a greeting, "Hello, sir. How are you?"

"I'm fine, thank you." The red-headed gentleman replied politely.

After they passed each other, Davis turned his head to glance back at the man with the long hair when at the same time the stranger twisted his head to get another look at Davis. Both instantly spun their heads back in the direction they were walking.

Davis hurried to his Jeep, took his cell out of his pocket. It was crucial that he tell Charley about this as soon as possible. "Charley, he's here!" Davis's voice revealed his excitement.

"Who's there? And where is there?" Charley asked. "Calm down and tell me what's going on."

"It's the Cowardly Lion. He's here at the Hotel behind the BP station. He fits the description perfectly, and he's driving an old black Cadillac."

"You mean the guy who was spotted at Spring Bank the day Devan was killed, and the next day broke into Janie's house?"

"That's the one. He's here at the hotel," Davis told him.

"You go on home. I'll check it out."

"I suggest you get out here right away. He may not stick around very long, I'll remain here till you arrive, just in case," Davis stated.

"Don't tell me how to do my job. I told you to go home, and I'll be out there as soon as I finish what I'm doing. It'll be less than fifteen minutes, and I don't want to see you there when I arrive."

"Okay," Davis responded to his insistent friend. "Tell me what you find out." Against his better judgement, he started the Jeep, pulled out of the parking lot and turned toward home.

***

Deidre opened the trunk lid to get the groceries out of her car at precisely the instant Davis pulled into the drive. "You got here just in time," she said. When he was standing nearby, she loaded grocery bags into his arms. "Did you successfully take care of your errands?" she asked suspiciously, looking at her husband's face.

"Everything is taken care of," Davis answered. With each loaded to the hilt, they were able to get all the groceries inside with one trip. Deidre put the meat and produce away first, before putting boxed and canned foods in their proper places.

"I need to take these things I picked up for Barbara over to her," Deidre told her husband, holding up the one bag that had not been stored away. "I'll be back shortly."

Davis nodded. "Take your time, Honey." he said.

Deidre had adored Barbara Mason since she had been in her teens, when the charming lady, now only a couple of years away from retirement, had been her preacher's wife in South Georgia. "Grocery delivery," Deidre announced, holding up the bag when Barbara came to her door.

"Nothing like instant service." Barbara smiled while reaching for her purchase. "How much do I owe you?" She asked.

"Round it off at eighteen dollars," Deidre told her friend.

Barbara reached for her purse and took out a ten, a five, and three ones and handed them to Deidre. "That ought to do it."

Deidre took the money and said, "Looks perfect. That's my mad money for next week."

"Sit down for a few minutes. We haven't had time to visit much recently."

"Just for a few minutes," "Deidre told her. "I promised Davis I would be back shortly."

"Oh, he can survive without you for ten or fifteen minutes," Barbara assured her. "How's Davis getting along these days?"

"The doctor says he's doing fine, but I don't know. It seems to me something is on his mind. You know, it was he and Janie that found that poor man dead the other day and you have seen first-hand how he is prone to jump in with both feet in such matters. Despite what he says, I think he can't let that go. But that's Davis, and I guess I'll just have to trust the Lord to see him through such ordeals."

"I think that's the right attitude. It's not doing anyone any good to fret over it when God is completely sufficient."

"I know that, but when I see how he's doing himself harm, it's hard to let go. Sometimes, he can be a rather stubborn man," Deidre declared.

"Like most men," Barbara laughed. "He's probably doing himself far less harm than what you think. Just let him be himself," Barbara recommended to her longtime friend who was still a newlywed. "How's Janie holding up in her bereavement?"

"Naturally, it's hard for her, especially since that lady from California showed up claiming to be Devan's fiancé. I think she doesn't know whether to mourn or be angry. You can understand the confusion such a situation can cause."

"Did she travel to the funeral?" Barbara asked.

"No, she stayed home for obvious reasons, and it was a difficult day for her. I was told she cried all day."

"We need to love on her and help her get through it, but most of all we must pray for her."

"I've already done a great deal of that. Davis says she plans to be back at work when the 1902 Stock Exchange opens on Tuesday," Deidre announced.

"That's probably best for her. You know what they say about staying busy. Do the police have any idea about who shot him?" Barbara asked.

"I don't know much about it, but they seem to be looking for a man with long red hair who was seen in the vicinity, and according to Davis, Devan was involved with his sister in a bitter fight over the family estate. It also has been suggested that the fiancé was awfully upset at him as was Janie's mother who thought he might take Janie away from her."

"Sounds like a highly complicated matter," Barbara surmised.

The two teachers talked about school for a few minutes before Deidre got up to return to her side of the house. *What a blessing to have Barbara right next door,* she told herself as she returned to her living room. She could faintly hear Davis stationed in the kitchen talking on his phone.

***

"If you don't tell me which room he's in, Mrs. Lawson, I will knock on every door in this hotel until I find him." Charley, in uniform, talked as if he meant business.

"Okay, he's in room 12, but I'm going to hold you responsible. My husband, Steve, knows Chief Hanson, and I promise you, this will be reported."

"You go right ahead and report it, Mrs. Lawson. That's the proper thing to do."

Charley looked at the door numbers as he briskly made his way down the hallway until he came to room number twelve and knocked.

"Who's there?" someone on the inside asked after a brief silence.

"You don't know me, but my name's Charley Nelson."

"What do you want, Charley Nelson?"

"I need to see you. Shouldn't take but a minute."

Charley heard the click of the door being unlocked before it opened. When he saw the man standing in front of him he thought, *He's right. He does look like the Cowardly Lion!*

It must've been Charley's uniform that spooked him. In three or four quick strides the red-headed man gained enough momentum to knock the smaller Charley against the door across the hallway. He was several paces down the hallway before Charley, who had been caught by surprise, began his chase. By the time the pair went past Jenny and a flabbergasted couple at the check in desk, Charley was closing in. They barely got to the edge of the parking lot when Charley, less than ten years removed from an outstanding career on the Adairsville Tiger football team, dove at the figure in front of him, causing both to skid on the pavement, The Lion was down, and, obviously, the fall had knocked the breath out of him. He was on his stomach grunting. Charley, pouncing on the back side of his prey, reached to his belt for handcuffs, pulling both his prisoner's hands behind him and snapping the cuffs. He got up and pulled the red-headed man, who was still making odd sounds, to his feet.

"Oh, stop your bellyaching," Charley told him, "You're not hurt."

"Not hurt!" The red-headed man all but screamed. "You just wait. I'll sue you for everything you're worth," he shouted at Charley. "I think my arm's broken and look, my good pants are torn at the knee, and I'm bleeding. Probably have internal injuries," he added as an afterthought.

The red-headed man continued to whine as Charley pulled him toward the patrol car where he opened the back door. "Ouch," he cried out as he was placed in the seat. "You don't have to be so rough."

"And you didn't have to run," Charley told him. "If you would have calmly responded to my inquiry, you wouldn't have those scrapes and scratches." Charley could hear him, still mumbling in the back seat when he got under the steering wheel.

Before starting his vehicle, Charley used his radio to contact the station. "Katie, is the chief available?"

"He's right here beside my desk," the dispatcher replied. "Hang on and I'll let you talk with him."

"Chief, I'm out at the Magnuson Hotel. I've got the red-headed guy who drives the black Caddy. He ran when I tried to talk with him, so I've got him cuffed in my back seat."

"You mean the guy Sheriff Wilson wants for questioning in the Devan Rhodes case?" Chief Hanson asked.

"One and the same," Charley told him.

"How did you find him?" the chief asked.

"It's a long story. I'll put it all in my report. The fact is, we had a little help."

"Davis Morgan, I bet," the chief offered a guess.

"You got it," Charley responded. "Whatever else you might say about the guy, he does have a good pair of eyes."

"I suppose he does, but he's got to learn to stay out of police business," Chief Hanson answered.

You ought to be grateful for the times he's pulled your fat out of the fire, Charley wanted to reply, but he didn't. "Do you want me to run him on down to the county jail?" Charley asked.

"No, bring him by here. I think I would like to question him before we give him to the guys down there."

"I'll do it, sir, but Sheriff Wilson isn't going to like it since it's their case." Charley advised his boss.

"I know, but he's our prisoner. Bring him on by here," Hanson insisted.

"I'll be there in five minutes," Charley responded.

Before he started the car, Charley took his personal cell phone from his pocket and called Davis. "I've got him," he told his anxious friend. "Hanson wants me to deliver him to the station, says he wants to question him. I guess he will spend a few hours in our holding cell before we surrender him to the county boys."

Davis spoke a couple of words before Charley broke in, "Got to go. The chief is expecting me at the station. Can't disappoint the boss, you know."

CHAPTER 11

Sunday morning worship was an exciting event for Davis. The preacher's message was superb. After hearing Clark preach for only a little more than a month, Davis was convinced they had a preacher who gave them more than fluff. Content was his strong point, but neither was he short on delivery. Today's sermon entitled, *The Joy of Walking with Christ*, was, in Davis's mind, close to a masterpiece. He, for one, was tremendously happy with their new South Carolina preacher. The best part of the day was that at the end of the service, there were four baptisms with all the candidates coming from the same family. The family unit consisted of two adults—a sharp looking couple, and two children. Davis guessed the young lady to be around twelve years old and the boy a little older, obviously a teenager. They, no doubt, would be delightful additions to the church.

Davis was also pleased to see Charley and Tonya come into the worship center to be seated on the next to last pew as the congregation was standing to sing the first worship song. Over the past three months, Charley had often been in the services when he was not on duty, and he sometimes brought Tonya with him. Davis had been praying for Charley's decision to give his life to the Lord, and for two years, he had taken every opportunity to speak to him on that subject, trying not to be a nuisance. Davis was convinced his low-key approach was having a positive effect on his friend. However, he had been concerned over the last few days that the condition in which he recently discovered the sometimes rather sensitive young man, along with his personal problems, might trigger a setback. But here he was, and Tonya was with him. Davis couldn't be more pleased.

After the service, Davis hurried to the back to catch Charley before he got away. Charley, with Tonya holding his arm, was already outside on the sidewalk before Davis got to him. "Where you headed in such a hurry?" Davis called out to his friend who always seemed to be moving a little faster than everyone else. "I need to talk with you."

"That's why I was in a hurry. I figured you would want to talk."

"I'm hurt that you don't have time for me. I thought we were good friends."

"It's not that. The problem is that you have a way of discreetly pumping me for information you have no business knowing. I'm talking about police matters," Charley added.

"You know I would never ask you to tell me anything that should be confidential," Davis replied.

"Yea, I know that like I know what the stock market is going to do tomorrow." Charley shot back with a chuckle. "The only times I've been reprimanded by the chief were all for telling you the particulars of certain cases."

"Well, I do have a couple of questions about the red-headed man you took into custody yesterday. I don't expect you to tell me anything that is supposed to be hush-hush."

"Go ahead and ask your questions. I'll tell you what I can," Charley reluctantly told him. "Since you are the person who found the body, as well as the party who gave us the tip that led to his capture, I guess you have a right to the basic facts."

"Has he been delivered to the county lockup?" Davis asked.

"He was taken to Cartersville last night after the chief questioned him."

"I'm curious about who he is," Davis stated.

"His name is Jon Greenleaf. He's a sorry excuse for a private investigator from Columbia, South Carolina. It's a miracle he's been able to hold onto his license. This is all I'm going to tell you about the current case, but while he denies shooting Devan, he admits that he had been hired to find a particular item."

"Hired by whom?" Davis asked.

"Can't tell you that," Charley sternly declared.

Davis could make a pretty good guess about the answer to that question. It had to be Devan's sister who hired him to find the lost will, or perhaps do away with Devan if the will could not be found. Devan's death eliminated her problem, leaving her as the only heir. "Did he deny breaking into Janie's house?" Davis inquired.

"I don't think Chief Hanson would mind me telling you that Greenleaf confesses to all the break ins and even admits he found Devan, already dead, and searched him for the item he was hired to find. He also claims that, when he was on his way to Cartersville recently, someone took a shot at him."

"Do you think he's telling the truth?" Davis asked

"I don't know," Charley answered. "It all falls together pretty neatly, but he's just the kind of scum that could be hired to eliminate someone's problem by murdering the source of the difficulty. If he is the shooter, there's another villain out there. Someone hired him to do it."

At that moment Tonya, who had been standing ten feet away talking with Deidre, returned to Charley's side. "Great to see you here today," Davis smiled at the short-haired beauty.

"I enjoyed it," she replied. "I like your new preacher."

"So, do I," Davis responded.

"Did Charley tell you about Miss Helen's house?" Tonya asked.

"No, what about Miss Helen's house?" Davis anxiously queried.

"She's putting it up for sale, and I'm scheduled to go with the agent this afternoon to look at it," Charley answered.

"Where's Miss Helen going to live?" Davis asked, suddenly concerned about his longtime friend.

"Miss Helen has decided it's time for her to move into an assisted living facility. She's been looking at places in both Rome and Cartersville as possibilities." Charley told him.

"Emotionally, it's going to be hard for her. That's the family home, and I think she's lived there for almost ninety years, all told. She moved out when she married, but she was widowed after only a few years. She then moved back in with her father and mother. The lady has been there ever since." Davis explained. "Why would you want that big house? It's definitely a fixer-upper and will require a lot of money and time to restore it."

"I know, but I may need more room down the road." Charley looked at Tonya and grinned. Her face was immediately transformed into a huge smile.

Davis turned toward Tonya and then Charley before asking, "Is there something I need to know?"

"Not yet," Charley grinned. "But stay tuned. There may be an announcement sometime in the future."

"I live in optimistic anticipation," Davis declared. "When or if there is any important news from you two, I expect to be among the first to know."

Charley only laughed before taking Tonya's hand and walking toward the parking lot. "Have a good afternoon and try to stay out of trouble," he called back to his friend.

"Me, trouble?" Davis responded. "I don't know what trouble is."

"Obviously not," Charley called out. "If you did, you would do a better job of staying away from it."

Usually Davis and Deidre went out to lunch with Jay and Amy on Sundays with Barbara often joining them. Today, Amy decided she needed to go home to rest. They would pick up chicken at Zaxby's to carry home with them. Barbara was in Cartersville where she had gone with two friends. They attended an early service at one of the large churches there and would take in an event at one of the theaters in that city. Davis and Deidre decided they would go home and reheat some leftovers. Neither of them felt very hungry.

***

After lunch, Davis sat down and turned on the TV to watch the Atlanta Braves play the New York Mets. By the fourth inning he was in deep slumber and didn't awake until there were two outs in the top of the eighth. Deidre took a brief nap before getting out some school work. One more week and she wouldn't have to be concerned about such things for over two months. Summer vacation was right around the corner.

It was late afternoon when Davis mentioned the giant oak tree at Spring Bank where he had found Devan. "I've heard people talk about Spring Bank ever since I've lived in Adairsville, but I've never been there," Deidre told her husband.

"I can't believe you, a history teacher, have never visited one of the most historical sites in North Georgia. Did you know it was in the house at Spring Bank that Confederate General Wofford and Federal General Judah met in May of 1865 to arrange the terms for surrender of seven thousand soldiers, the last Confederate forces in Georgia?"

"No, I didn't have any idea," Deidre, obviously impressed, responded.

"You know, we could be there in ten or twelve minutes. There's no time like the present. Let's take a drive out there," Davis suggested.

"Do you think we have time? It's not long until dark."

"We've got plenty of time," Davis assured her.

In less than fifteen minutes, Deidre's eyes were glued to the extensive terraced spot beside the spring where the Spring Bank Plantation House once stood. "It's beautiful!" she remarked. "But it's sort of sad in the twilight of the evening."

"I would say kind of spooky." Davis pointed toward the turkey buzzards perched on limbs around the site. There must have been thirty of the ugly, black birds congregated in that one small spot. "Combine the evening shadows with the buzzards and it's pretty eerie."

Davis parked the Jeep. "Let's go in that direction, and I'll show you the family cemetery," Davis remarked pointing toward the southwest.

"How far is it?" Deidre asked.

"It's just a short distance. There are only forty acres of the original nine hundred being preserved, so it only takes a jiffy to get to anything on the site."

Deidre took Davis's hand as they walked. "Is that the big oak tree?" Deidre asked facing east where she could see a huge tree with yellow crime tape strung around it.

"That's it," Davis confirmed. "Look at that trunk and the size of the crown. I'm amazed every time I see it. Majestically standing there near the creek, it always makes me think of that passage in Psalm one that says of the faithful man, *He is like a tree planted by streams of water...*

"In what way is the faithful person like a tree?" the always inquisitive Deidre asked.

"I tell you what, if I ever get to preach again, I'll do a sermon on that topic. I don't believe I've done that before."

"What do you mean, if you get to preach again? Of course, you'll preach again. It would be a crime to keep a preacher as capable as you out of the pulpit indefinitely."

"Thank you, honey. You're sweet to say that, but maybe you're just a little biased."

They could see the small, fenced spot up ahead despite the darkness that was starting to cover the wooded area. "How many graves are there?" Deidre asked as they drew near to their destination.

"Ten," Davis answered. "Nine family members and one family friend."

"Who's the friend that made it to the family plot?" Deidre asked. "He or she must have been pretty well regarded to receive that honor. Deidre looked toward the bushes to her right and reached for Davis's hand.

"Don't worry, honey. That's just a rabbit or some other small animal rustling the bushes over there. The answer to your question is one of the most interesting stories out here. That grave contains the remains of an artist by the name of Everett B.D. Julio who knocked on the door one evening and stayed until the end of his life. He did the famous painting sometimes called, *The Last Meeting of Lee and Jackson*. It's a fascinating story. Remind me when we get home, and I'll dig out the article I saved that discloses all the details."

Deidre abruptly squeezed Davis's hand tightly. "Davis there's something or someone over there in the bushes. I see something white." She spoke with almost a quiver in her voice.

"It's nothing, honey. I know your eyesight's better than mine, but I don't see a thing. Let's walk in that direction, and you'll see."

"I don't know, Davis. Maybe we ought to stay here." Deidre held her ground.

Suddenly a white figure came through the bushes headed full steam in their direction. Deidre yelled, "Davis!" before she embraced him as tightly as he had ever been squeezed, hiding her head on his chest. "Do something, Davis!" She screamed. "Do something!"

Davis wondered what he could do, being so tightly wrapped up by his wife's arms.

CHAPTER 12

The white four-legged creature standing about three feet tall ran past no more than a yard to their right. Another animal, identical but for being a little shorter, scampered close behind the first. "Goats!" Davis bellowed. "It's two goats! Look, Honey, it's only goats," Davis declared with a note of relief in his voice. He tried to turn Deidre in the direction of the sprinting animals, but she continued to hold on tight while slightly turning her head to catch a glimpse of the pair of runaway domesticated creatures.

"I don't seem to be able to keep those critters in the pasture. I hope they didn't scare you folks." The voice that originated from a man wearing a green cap coming out of the bushes was familiar to Davis.

"Seems like you have a hard time keeping all your livestock behind fences, Doug." It was Doug Touchstone whose cows had been loose on the day of the murder.

"I've got a lot of fence. Keeping an eye on it and maintaining the whole lot isn't an easy job for one old, worn out gent with a thousand other things to do," The farmer whined. "Maybe you'd like to have a job. I could use a good hand."

"No, sir, I think I have all I can handle, though farm work might be enjoyable."

"You stay at it for a week or two, and you won't think it so enjoyable. Don't think there is any work more demanding," the farmer declared.

Deidre finally let go of her grip on Davis. "Deidre, this is Doug Touchstone, a new friend I met just recently. Doug, this is my wife, Deidre."

Doug removed his cap to reveal a head with little hair on top. Holding his cap in his left hand, he reached with his right to take Deidre's hand. "You're a pretty little thing. He must have something going for him or maybe a lot of money to hook a lady like you." Doug offered with a serious expression on his face while nodding toward Davis.

"He's got a lot going for him, but it's not money," Deidre answered with a chuckle.

"Say, Doug, I've been wanting to talk with you. I thought of another question about the day of the murder out here," Davis took a couple of steps toward the farmer who was placing his cap back on his head. "Were you out on Hall Station Road any during an hour or so before you pulled in here that day?"

Doug took a moment to stare into space while he tried to recall. "Yes, I was. I worked on the fence that was down beside the highway for at least a half hour."

"Was that between here and Adairsville? Davis asked.

"Yes, I guess it was about a half mile in that direction," Mr. Touchstone answered.

"Did a lot of north-bound traffic pass by while you were out there?"

"As I remember, it was about like usual. A car went by about every minute or two."

"Do you remember anything unusual about any of those cars that passed?" Davis probed.

"No, I don't think so, but probably more than half the traffic wasn't cars at all. I remember a lot of pickups. That's probably not uncommon. A lot of the fellas living out this way drive pickups," Doug added. "I do remember that crazy old lady, what's her name?" he looked up as if trying to draw the name out of the sky.

"Rita, Rita Edison. I think that's her name. I waved at her, but she turned her nose up at me and looked the other way."

Davis knew that Rita had driven Janie's car to Rome that day and probably had taken the route through Kingston to get home, but he also knew she had not arrived back home until a good deal later. He wondered about the time frame and made a mental note to ask Mrs. Edison about it.

"Do you recall anything else, no matter how small, about the traffic that day? Davis asked.

"Don't think so. It was pretty normal."

"I assume you've talked with Sheriff Wilson." Davis stated the obvious.

"Yeah, he came by the house the other day and took up about two hours of my valuable work time. I better get over there while Sadie and Fred are busy playing in the creek or they may get away again." Doug pointed toward the two goats, that could barely be seen in the rapidly falling darkness, at the edge of the creek.

"Good to see you again Doug. I'll think about that job offer. I may need one soon."

"You do that, son," the farmer said as he walked toward his two ornery head of livestock.

"He seems like a nice man," Deidre remarked.

"You're just saying that because he called you a pretty little thing."

"The least you can say about him is that he has good eyes," Deidre responded with a giggle.

"Tell me," Davis asked. "Why did you continue to hang on to me so tightly even after we saw that it was only goats coming toward us? I think you just wanted an excuse to cozily snuggle up to me."

"I don't need an excuse to do that. No, when you said *goat*, I thought you said *ghost*," Deidre said sheepishly.

***

All the businesses in the 1902 Stock Exchange, including the Corra Harris Bookshop were always locked up tight all day on Monday. Often, Davis used this day to travel out of town on one of his treasure hunts. The search for significant stock was still Davis's favorite responsibility related to the book business, but today he decided to stay in town. There were a couple of people he wanted to see. After doing yard work most of the morning, Davis went inside for a shower before making himself a sandwich and digging out some chips from the bottom of the cupboard where Deidre often put the salty foods, thinking he would be less likely to find them in that spot.

He turned on the TV while he was eating to watch the noon news, but soon became discouraged with that. He went into the kitchen to wash the small serving plate, glass, and table knife he used to spread the mustard on his sandwich before leaving the house.

Davis found Janie and her mother home when he arrived at their place. Janie opened the door for him. "It's good to see you, Mr. Book Man. I actually miss you when we are away from each other two or three days."

"And I have missed you," Davis replied. "It's just not the same when I don't have someone around to hassle me." Davis embraced his young friend. "I've been thinking a lot about you. How're you doing?"

"Better," Janie answered. "I'm ready to get back to work tomorrow."

"We're ready to have you back. Pam is a fine lady and a hard worker, but she's not Janie."

"What about you, Mrs. Edison? How are you doing?" Davis inquired. "I guess it's been neat having Janie home these few days?"

"*Neat* isn't the word I would use," the older lady replied. "All she's done the past week is sit around and whimper. I'm glad she's going back to work. I can't get anything out of her around here."

Obviously, Janie hasn't received much compassion and encouragement at home. When she gets back to work, we'll make sure she's loved on and adequately supported.

"While I'm thinking about it, Mrs. Edison, let me ask you about your trip to Rome the day we found Devan. I thought you might have seen something on your way home. You did come back through Kingston, didn't you?"

"Yes, I always use that way these days with all the construction on the other road."

"What time was it when you went past Spring Bank?" Davis asked.

"Oh, I don't know. I guess it was sometime between three-thirty and four." Mrs. Edison stuttered.

"That must have been about the time Devan was shot. Did you see anything out of the ordinary there?" Davis asked.

"No, I didn't pay any attention."

"Did you see Doug Touchstone repairing one of his fences beside the road?" Davis inquired.

"Yes, I saw the old creep. Tried to flirt with me, but I stopped that right away."

"One more question. It was much later when you got home. Where were you between that time and the time you arrived home?"

"I don't know, let me see. As I remember I went by Food Lion for some groceries, and then to Dollar General, and then out to Fred's before I got home"

Davis noticed that Mrs. Edison was getting a little nervous and maybe somewhat irritated with him and thus decided it would be best to discontinue the questions.

They spent the next few minutes visiting, but Mrs. Edison didn't have much to say, and occasionally Davis noticed her looking intently at him, sort of suspiciously.

***

After his visit with Janie and her mom, Davis drove the half mile to Miss Helen's place. Miss Helen had been his friend since he was a child, and even then, he thought she was ancient. Everyone knew she was well into her nineties and some argued she had passed the century mark. Though she didn't get around very well anymore, it seemed to Davis that, despite what Mayor Sam said about her, her mind was almost as sharp as it had always been. It was her knowledge of local history that Davis found fascinating and often useful.

After going up the three steps to get to the big porch that he walked across to get to the door, Davis knocked loudly. In previous visits, he discovered the doorbell, which probably was installed at least seventy years ago, was out of order. Miss Helen's evaluation of that was that, since people didn't visit anymore, they didn't need doorbells.

Davis stepped back and waited after knocking. He knew it would take Miss Helen some time to get to the door. After a minute or two he heard her voice. "I'm coming, just takes me awhile," she called out. Shortly thereafter, Miss Helen appeared at the door dressed as if she were going to church on Sunday morning, but then, that is how she was always dressed when in public or when company came. "It's good to see you preacher." Even though Davis had not held down a fulltime ministry now for some time, he would eternally be Preacher to her.

"Since you called ahead, I've got your sweet tea ready," she told him pointing toward a glass sitting on a white cloth napkin on top of a small end table beside the chair where Davis knew she prefer he sit when he was there. "I've been thinking about you," she said. "I've been wondering how your heart is holding up."

"The doctor told me recently, Miss Helen, that everything is still looking good."

"Then I suspect you'll be back in the pulpit before long," she said more as a statement than a question.

"Maybe," Davis told her. "But I'm going to have to find a church that is willing to take on a worn-out parson with a weak ticker."

"There are a lot of churches around here that would be glad to have you as their preacher."

"Thank you for the kind words, Miss Helen. I hear you're getting ready to make some changes. Charley Nelson tells me you are selling the house to take up residence in one of those fancy places in Rome or Cartersville."

"Yes, I think it's time. I can hardly get up those steps to my porch any longer. Not only that, but I'm lonely," Miss Helen declared. "I've lived much of my life right here in this house alone, but it's not like it used to be. People used to visit all the time. But for you and a couple of other people, I don't see anyone anymore. Most of my old friends are gone, and the younger folks just don't have time to visit. I'll be better off where I have people to talk with."

"Have you made any decisions about where you're going?" Davis asked his elderly friend.

"I think it's going to be Rome. There's a place there I like a lot, and if we can work out the financial details, that's probably where I'll go. You'll still visit me when I get over there, won't you?"

"You can be sure of that," Davis replied. "Where would I get my information about Adairsville's past if I didn't get it from you. That reminds me, what do you think of the movie crew in here making that *Great Locomotive Chase* movie?"

"Well, at least they've got the place right this time. I just hope they get the story correct," Miss Helen replied.

"You never know about these Hollywood people," Davis spoke. "They're more interested in entertainment than getting the history right."

"Incidentally, Miss Helen. I was wondering what you may know about Rita Edison. Anything you might be able to tell me about her?"

"You're talking about Rita Monroe. Monroe was her family name. I don't know much about her except that she was pretty wild when she was younger. As a teenager, she was in and out of trouble constantly, but I think she grew out of it. I really haven't heard anything about her in years."

"I was just wondering," Davis told her. "Her daughter Janie is the clerk at the 1902 Stock Exchange. Deidre and I are extremely fond of her."

It was over an hour before Davis could get away from Miss Helen. He was glad he had taken the time to stop by. He felt sadness about Miss Helen having to leave her home, but thankful that she would be in a place where she would be looked after and enjoy companionship. Sometimes Davis despised change, but he knew there was no way to stop it.

CHAPTER 13

It looked like a team huddle on the walk, in front of the 1902 Stock Exchange. The old quarterback, Bobby Thorton, as well as Police Chief Bob Hanson, newcomer Bertram Shaw, and Mayor Sam Ellison were all standing with Davis in an imperfect circle, each anxious for his turn to eloquently expound on a subject that was near to his heart, at least on this day, at this place.

"If these movie companies keep coming to town, some guidelines will have to be established." Mr. Shaw glanced toward the Mayor and then at Chief Hanson.

"Amen," Bobby spoke up. "They shouldn't be allowed to box everything in whenever they want without warning. I bet Davis hasn't done a hint of business since they've been in town. Nobody can get to his shop."

"I haven't done a whole lot more than a *hint* of business since I opened the shop," Davis said with a smile.

"It's all new to us. We'll learn from this little adventure and get it right next time. I can assure you of that," the mayor declared.

"Speaking of the movie project, have you guys caught the murderer of that young man shot down toward Kingston?" Bertram Shaw addressed Bob Hanson.

"We aren't involved with that investigation. It comes under the jurisdiction of the county authorities. But I am happy to report that, with our help, they've detained a suspect." The tone of the Chief's voice left no doubt he was proud of the part his department played in the capture.

"It wasn't one of our citizens," the mayor quickly pointed out. "He came from out of town."

"Our citizens are all law-abiding," Bob said sarcastically, before everyone laughed.

"Well, if this meeting is over, I've got some work to do at the office. My daughter gave me tickets for the Braves game for my birthday. I don't want to be late," Sam told them.

"There's a good idea for an outing sometime. Let's plan to get a group of guys together and go to a ballgame," Bobby suggested. "Football's my favorite, but a baseball game, especially with the fellas, can be a lot of fun."

"Count me out," Chief Hanson responded. "For me, baseball has always been about as much fun as watching paint dry. I'm a NASCAR fan myself. I love the excitement of a good race."

"I like racing too, but I guess there aren't many sports I don't like. I've even been known to go to a wrestling match from time to time," Bobby told the group as they were disbanding.

Davis was pleased to see Janie behind the checkout desk when he entered the building that housed his bookshop. "Looks like the meeting of the city council has dismissed for the day," Janie joked.

Davis was glad to hear Janie sounding a little more like herself. "There was no reason to continue the summit," he told her. "All problems were resolved."

"I know better than that. That group may create a lot of difficulties, but I doubt they will come up with many solutions," Janie teased. "I saw a lot of brawn out there, but not an abundance of brain power. Present company excluded, of course," she said glancing over at Davis.

"Janie, I hate to bring it up, and I promise you I won't keep doing so, but I need to ask you about Devan's sister. Did he talk about her?"

"Not much," Janie answered. "I know they were arguing over a family matter. Sometimes, after he talked with her, he would be riled up for a while."

"Do you know what the disagreement was about?" Davis asked.

"I think it mostly had to do with the fact that their mother was troubled by Devan giving her so little attention. She cut him out of her will before she died, but Devan told me that was no longer a problem," Janie stated.

"Did he tell you why it was no longer an issue?"

"No. He only said he had it covered," Janie responded.

"Did he give you any indication of how his relationship with his sister was before this dispute occurred," Davis probed.

"I got the impression they had always been close. I think she was a couple of years older than him and maybe tended to be a little bossy where he was concerned. Several times he told me amusing stories from their childhood and teen years. I think they were probably the typical brother and sister. Even though I never met her, I would be awfully surprised if she had anything to do with his death," Janie added. "I thought they caught the man responsible."

"The suspect they caught may or may not have done the shooting, but if he did, it was because he was hired by someone," Davis explained while turning to walk back to his shop. "Thank you for the information, Janie."

With only a couple of customers, the morning moved slowly for Davis. He spent much of his time sitting in an uncomfortable chair reading a Nero Wolff novel. "Is that what you do all day," the voice was a deep one that Davis knew well.

"Hi, Dean. What're you up to? I know you're not here to buy books."

"No, I haven't bought a book since I purchased my last comic book when I was in middle school. But Sherrie brings home enough of those dumb romance stories to keep the whole town supplied," The big man sounded a little disgusted. "I was passing by on my way to City Hall and thought I'd stop in to check on you."

"Well, welcome to my world. It's nice of you to drop in. It shortens my day when a friend comes by for a visit," Davis explained.

"I guess the real reason I'm here is to thank you. I know we joke and go on at each other a lot, but, Davis, I do appreciate how you quietly help so many of our crowd. It seems you're always there with the right words or a helping hand. When you decided to become a pastor, you chose the right profession."

"To be honest Dean, I didn't choose to become a pastor. The whole idea scared the living daylights out of me. The Lord called me. He didn't give me a choice."

"Regardless of how it happened, it suits you well. You've done wonders with my brother. I don't know what you said to him the other day, but I know after your conversation with him, he's back on the right track again. I understand, as a big brother, I'm the one who ought to be there for him, but it's been you more than anyone else who's seen him through the tough times the last couple of years."

"Charley's my friend—my closest friend other than my wife. You know I was an only child. When I was a kid, I was always searching to find that brother, that best friend, who would put up with me and stand with me in every situation. I always had a desperate need for someone like that, and maybe you will recall there were several of those while we were growing up. I guess that basic desire for a brother went with me into my adult years, and that role was often filled by leaders in the churches I served in Richmond and later in Indianapolis. Charley, though thirteen or fourteen years younger than me, has become that brother over these past two years. And it's been a two-way street. He's made a significant contribution to my life, and in his sometimes unconventional way has helped me through some of my worst times. He's a good man and ultimately would have worked himself through this latest crisis even without any encouragement from me. I hope you realize that you haven't failed Charley in any way. He looks up to you, and I think, now that his dad is gone, he sees you more as a father than a big brother. You've had a major impact on his life," Davis assured his friend.

"I hope that's true, but it seems to me that in the ways that really count, you've been the man," Dean surmised.

"No person's contribution to another's life is minor. It takes the influence of many people to make a man a man," Davis stated. "You were pouring your life into Charley's long before I knew him."

"Anyway, thank you," Dean uttered warmly to his longtime friend. "You're appreciated, man."

Davis knew how hard it was for Dean to make such a serious speech, and he felt unworthy of the praise. Perhaps he had learned to cover it well, but the truth was, he often wrestled with feelings of inadequacy and sometimes thought of himself as a total failure. "Thank you for your kindness," Davis responded to Dean, thinking he should say more to enable his friend to know how much he helped him with his gracious remarks, but instead left it there. Davis followed him to the door. "Behave yourself," he called out to the big man. "I'd hate to have to come and bail you out of jail."

"You did that once, didn't you? You don't have to worry about that anymore. I've now got some pull down at the jailhouse," he shouted back at Davis, causing an older lady strolling down the walkway to turn and look his way.

Later in the day, Davis gave Charley a call. "Hey, how's your day been?" He asked the young policeman.

"Not bad," Charley responded. "I haven't had to arrest even one person today."

"How will you ever meet your quota at that rate?" Davis joked. "I thought I would make a couple of requests regarding the Devan Rhodes case." He now spoke almost shyly.

"I'll listen to what you have to say, but you need to know that the chief's been on my back about that case. He told me, in no uncertain terms, that it belongs to the Sheriff's Department, and besides that, it's all but closed with the arrest of the P.I.," Charley told him.

"Maybe he's right, but I'm convinced there's more to it," Davis explained. "If Jon Greenleaf is guilty, someone ordered the hit, and I'm not even one hundred percent sure he did the shooting."

"I share your reservations. So, what do you want me to do about it?" Charley asked.

"Two things. First, would it be possible for you to get the newspaper accounts from fifteen years ago faxed, emailed, or however they do it now to me? I'm talking about the accounts from Elbert County of the murder Devan witnessed."

"I think I can do that, though I'm taking a big risk. If the chief finds out, I'm a goner," Charley muttered. "What's the second thing that you want me to do, which is likely to get me terminated?"

"Would you arrange for me and you to visit with Greenleaf down at the county jail sometime this week when you're available?" Davis requested.

"Yeah, that's probably the one that will end my law enforcement career. I'll see what I can do, if you'll help me find a job when it's all over."

CHAPTER 14

D avis had taken the last bite of his sandwich only a couple of minutes before the phone in his pocket rang. "Davis, Bob Hanson. Could you stop by the station this afternoon? Something has happened you need to know about."

It puzzled Davis that the chief wanted to give him information, since he often lectured   Charley for being too free to pass police business on to him. *It probably has to do with the chaplain's responsibilities*, he decided. "Sure Chief, I've finished my lunch and am about to leave the house now. I can be there in about five minutes, if you're available."

"Come on by. I'll be waiting for you, Chief Hanson replied.

Hanson was sitting behind his desk when Davis entered. "Sit down, Davis. I've got some rather astonishing news for you."

Davis flopped into the chair in front of Hanson's desk, anxious to hear what the chief had to say. "I know you remember, Clive Garrett," Hanson stated.

Just hearing the man's name caused Davis's heart to skip a beat. "You bet I remember him. He's the Rat-Face Man, the hit man who did everything he could to kill me, the one who kidnapped Amy. Yes, I'll never forget him." Davis spoke with obvious revulsion.

"Well, I'm not happy to have to tell you he's on the loose. Maybe it's been on the news by now, I don't know. But the fact is, he escaped from the Ohio State Penitentiary in Youngstown yesterday. As I remember, he took exception to you taking a ball bat to him and bringing him back here from Fort Mountain in the trunk of your car. I recall him directing some pretty harsh threats toward you."

"How could that happen?" Davis questioned. "How can a dangerous animal like Garrett escape from a state prison with all the precautions and technology we have in today's world?"

"It occasionally happens," Bob replied. "I know it's hard to believe, but our prisons aren't one hundred percent escape proof. Since we were the arresting department, they sent me a report. It appears he and another man worked together to make a twenty-foot steel ladder to scale the prison fence while working in the prison's sheet metal shop. Their jobs there also gave them the ability to fashion a gun and a key. The report states the key was carved from memory after one of them saw an officer's copy. At the end of their exercise time, the two prisoners waited until the guards were busy, unlocked the door and walked out. They then cut a hole in the inner fence and scaled the outer fence with their ladder. They were gone before they were missed. Evidently someone was waiting near the penitentiary to drive them away."

"As disturbed as Garrett was at me, I question whether he can or would want to make his way here just to deal with me." Davis stated with a probing tone to his voice.

"My thoughts exactly," Chief Hanson replied. "There's a major manhunt in progress that'll soon pay dividends. It won't take them long to have him back behind bars."

Davis knew he would have to immediately tell Amy, who still had nightmares about her experience with this man and his partner. He didn't want her to get the news from the media. Being late in her pregnancy, this was news she didn't need. He would call her as soon as school was dismissed for the day.

***

Another day and another dollar was the thought lingering in Janie's mind when she locked the doors of the 1902 Stock

Exchange shortly after five o'clock. Davis and two other vendors left just ahead of her. Not wanting to go home just yet, she decided on the spur of the moment to drive to the Calhoun Walmart to pick up a few things. These were items that could be found here in Adairsville, but she reasoned the fifteen-minute drive to Calhoun would help clear her mind. She wasn't yet quite ready to face her mother. Hopefully, the drive would help prepare her for the evening.

Janie's mind was somewhere in the not too distant past as she drove toward her destination. She didn't notice the red sports car approaching her from the rear. With no traffic coming toward them at that moment, the driver of the sports car stomped on the accelerator, quickly moving about a half car length ahead of Janie's six-year-old vehicle. Janie caught a glimpse of the female driver just before she turned the steering-wheel toward her. The result was that Janie had to sharply whip the wheel to the right to avoid a crash. Her last thought before roughly bouncing across the wide ditch into the plowed field was, that woman has lost her mind. Since she was not traveling very fast and was now in the soft dirt of a recently plowed field, she came to a quick halt. She breathed a sigh of relief. Her quick self-inventory revealed she seemed to be without serious injuries. She was thankful she was using her seat belt.

Janie then saw the red sports car coming back in her direction, causing her to be completely immobilized by fear. When the small car reached a spot as close as the driver could get to her and still be in the road. The brunette behind the wheel stopped the car, rolled down the window and began to scream at Janie. She wasn't about to roll down her own windows. She was unable to distinguish the words of the woman, but she could clearly see she was irate about something. Janie was finally able to regain enough mental composure to lock her doors. The woman was still screaming as she drove away directing hand gestures toward the terrified young clerk.

Janie did not move for the next three or four minutes, looking back several times to make sure the mad woman in the red sports car was not again coming her way. Finally, she reached for her purse in the seat next to her and pulled out her cell phone. With her hands severely shaking, it took her three tries to punch 911.

***

Having to take care of some chores at home, it was mid-morning when Davis arrived at the 1902 Stock Exchange. He was surprised to see Pam back behind the checkout counter. "Is Janie not feeling well?" He asked the substitute clerk after cordially greeting her.

"I don't know," Pam answered. "I received a call asking me to fill-in today. I wasn't given an explanation as to why I was needed."

I'll wait until a little later to call and check on her, Davis decided. *If she is ill, she's probably resting.*

A half hour later Charley, not in uniform, came in with some papers in hand. "Did you hear what happened to Janie late yesterday?" He asked.

"No, I haven't. I wondered why Pam was subbing for her today. What happened?" Davis anxiously asked.

"Evidently, while driving to Calhoun after work she was run off the road by a crazy lady in a red sports car."

"Was she injured?" Davis apprehensively asked.

"No, she's somewhat shaken up, but the folks at Gordon Medical Center decided she had no injuries," Charley replied.

"So, she was in Gordon County when it happened?" Davis inquired.

"That's right. She called 911, and it was the Gordon County Sheriff's Department that responded. One of the officers who investigated is a friend of mine. I guess Janie, for some reason, mentioned to him she knew me. Later, he called to tell me about the incident."

"Was the crazy lady in the red sports car apprehended? Davis asked.

"No, evidently she turned around, stopped and yelled at Janie and then sped back toward Adairsville."

"I would jump to the conclusion that it was Devan's fiancée, the charming Caroline Robertson, if she were still in the area, but I assume she left to go to Devan's funeral," Davis suggested.

"You're right. She did travel to South Carolina for the service, but she has had plenty of time to return. The description my friend gave me sounded very much like her," Charley said. "I'm going to ask around. I would be willing to bet she's our girl."

"Do you think it was about her punishing Janie for spending time with Devan?" Davis asked.

"Could be. She seems to have that kind of disposition. It may have been an act of revenge, or it may have been something more," Charley surmised. "Incidentally, I've taken care of the two assignments you gave me. I have here in my hands a copy of the news reports of that murder that Devan witnessed fifteen years ago."

"Is there anything there that we didn't already know?" Davis asked.

"Not really, except a pretty good description of the killer that was given to the authorities by Devan and the other boys. The shooter was a little older than I was led to believe by the initial information. The boys said he was somewhere between forty and fifty. Here, I'll give these to you and you can go over them with a fine-tooth comb. Maybe you'll see something I missed," Charley told him while handing him the papers he had held in his right hand.

My second assignment was to arrange for us to talk with Jon Greenleaf. I'm working the night shift, so I've made an appointment for us to see Greenleaf today at two o'clock. Does that work for you?" Charley asked.

"I can make it work," Davis told him. "I have a favor to ask," Davis told his friend.

"Why does that not surprise me?" Charley responded.

"Don't tell my wife about us talking with Greenleaf," Davis requested.

"What's the matter? Have we become a little hen-pecked?" Charley teased.

"I just don't want her to worry," Davis responded.

"I guess I can understand that," Charley said, turning to head toward the door. "I'll pick you up here around one-thirty."

Davis knew he would get little done the rest of the day. When his mind was focused on a mystery, it was hard for him to concentrate on anything else. He sat in a small chair in his shop where he stayed until he read all the articles given to him by Charley. Later, he took his phone from his pocket and punched the button that would connect him with Janie. "Hello, Janie. I hear you had a little trouble yesterday..."

CHAPTER 15

"I assume you and Tonya have worked things out," Davis remarked to Charley, who was driving his vehicle south on Interstate 75 toward Cartersville.

"What makes you think that?" Charley asked.

"Well, the last two times I've seen you two together, you've looked more like you were mad for each other than mad at one another," Davis explained.

"We've talked several times. Even though I'm not pleased that she'll relocate to Jacksonville, I understand her position, and I'm trying to be civil about it. We're determined to make it work," Charley added.

"Good for you," Davis commended his friend. "How much time before she leaves? A week or so?" he guessed.

"That's about it. Actually, a couple of days less than that. There is, I'm glad to tell you, a development that gives me some hope that this will be only a temporary arrangement," Charley added.

"Oh, what's that?" Davis asked.

"Tonya's brother is currently dating someone he likes very much. She hasn't met her but feels this lady could be a good wife to her brother and stepmother for the girls. It's not going to happen in the next week or two, but Tonya has hopes the relationship, under the circumstances, might progress rapidly."

"That's good news. I, of course, don't know either of the two people involved, but I will make it a matter of prayer." Davis assured Charley.

I hope they don't push things too quickly because of the situation, was the thought running through Davis's mind. He decided it best to keep his apprehension to himself, but he would include his concern in his prayers.

"What are your thoughts about the Rat-Face Man? Do you think it's possible he'll come after me?" Davis asked.

"I don't know," Charley answered after a moment of silence. "Usually, the guys who escape are trying to find somewhere to hide. They're more interested in staying out of prison than getting revenge, but Garrett may be different. He strikes me as the kind of man that would cross land and sea to get even, and there is no doubt he was genuinely peeved at you. I don't think anyone had ever handled him as thoroughly as you did. It may be that he hasn't gotten over that. I'd watch my back if I were you."

"Thanks for the encouragement," Davis responded. "I was hoping you'd tell me there's no reason for me to worry."

"Just trying to help," Charley replied. "Lying to you isn't going to help."

"You're right. A lie never helped anyone."

Charley led the way when they reached the Bartow County Jail complex. After speaking to a couple of people Charley obviously knew, the two men were escorted to an interview room. Davis, having visited inmates in the past, knew this wasn't normal procedure for visitors, but presumed the VIP treatment was due to Charley being an active law enforcement officer.

They were seated. About five minutes later, Jon Greenleaf was brought in by a uniformed officer. "No! No way am I going to talk with you!" the prisoner said when he saw Charley across the table. "You're the little guy who critically injured me. I don't want anything to do with you."

"If I were you, I would sit down and cut the critically injured bit. It's to your advantage to cooperate with us," Charley told him.

"I'll sit and listen to what you have to say, but we'll see about the cooperation."

"That's fair enough. This is Davis Morgan," Charley said. He motioned toward Davis. "We've some questions to ask you. The best thing you can do for yourself is to cut the foolishness and tell us the truth. I know, at present, you are only charged with several break ins, but the fact is you're about this close to being charged with murder." Charley held up his right hand with his thumb and index finger about an inch apart. Most everyone in this building is convinced you shot and killed Devan Rhodes."

"I didn't shoot anyone," the shaggy haired prisoner yelled. "I admit I was hired to find an item, and I might have side stepped the law a little in looking for it, but I never killed anyone. My gun, for which I have a permit, has not been out of my glove compartment since I've been here. A guy took a shot at me, but I didn't even get it out then. I've pointed a gun toward no one since I've been here," he insisted.

"Okay, if that's true, there are some matters that need to be cleared up," Charley insisted.

"You said you were hired to find an item. What item, and who hired you?" Charley asked. The prisoner was silent, probably pondering whether to answer. "We can stop here and go home, and you will most likely be charged with murder or you can help us and there is a chance you will get only a few months for breaking and entering. It's your choice," Charley told him. "The best way to prove you're not guilty is to find the guilty party. It'll benefit you to help us do that."

"So, you believe me when I tell you I'm not guilty?" Greenleaf asked.

"Let's just say my mind is open. We want to find the truth," Charley informed him.

"All right, here's the story. I was hired by Jeanette Odon, Rhode's sister, to find and retrieve her mother's will which Rhodes stole."

"Why did she think Devan stole the will?" Davis asked.

"Because there is a pretty good bundle of money at stake, and with this latest will, the old lady disinherited Devan," Greenleaf answered. "A missing will benefitted no one but him."

"Wasn't the will on file in an attorney's office?" Charley inquired.

"Not this one. It was hand written just a few days before Mrs. Rhode's death. There were witnesses and such. It was legal, but in all the confusion when the old lady got so ill, it was never given to her lawyer," Greenleaf explained.

"Did you find the will? Davis asked.

"No, I didn't," he answered.

"Isn't it true that, with Devan dead, Mrs. Odon's problem was solved?" Davis probed.

"Yes, that's true. The fact is, she called me to tell me to go on home not a half hour before your pal here broke into my room and manhandled me. With Devan dead, she was the only heir. The will didn't matter. But, if you're saying that was motive for me to kill him, you're wrong! I've never killed anyone."

"I'm not saying you're guilty, but you have to admit it looks pretty bad for you." Charley inserted. "How'd the sister sound when she called you? I mean, about her brother's death? Did she seem upset that her brother was dead or maybe glad?"

"She was furious when she hired me. I thought then, she was ready to scratch out his eyeballs. When she called me after his death, she seemed sad, almost if there had been no trouble between them. I guess blood is thicker than water," he added.

"We have an eye witness who saw you leaving the vicinity where Devan was killed. Tell us about that." Davis requested.

"Yes, it's true, I was there. When I found out Devan was going out to what would probably be an isolated spot, I decided it would be a good time to confront him about the missing will. I had a little bit of a problem finding the exact spot, but when I saw an Adairsville police cruiser pull out into the highway, I figured that had to be the spot. He, no doubt, drove through, patrolling that space set aside for limited use."

"Did you see anyone else on your way in?" Charley asked.

"No. I saw Devan's rental car parked, so I got out of my car and walked around looking for him. I must have hiked around that place for at least ten minutes before I spotted a really big tree. It was still at a distance, but I could see that something was underneath. It didn't take me but a few seconds to figure out that what I saw was someone laying on his back on the ground. I hurried to that spot and found Devan. I saw the blood on his shirt, so I checked his pulse. There was no doubt about him being dead."

Greenleaf paused and sat silently before Davis asked, "What did you do then?"

"I searched his pockets to see if I could find the will," he admitted. "It never occurred to me that since he was dead, I didn't need it."

"Did you find it?" Charley inquired.

"I did not," he answered.

"Did you take anything from his pockets? Davis asked.

"Certainly not," the prisoner responded. "What do you think I am, a thief?"

"Well, you were breaking into houses and motel rooms. One might assume you had those tendencies," Charley charged.

"Those break ins, as you call them, were me doing my job. I was only looking for the will and took absolutely nothing when I couldn't find what I was after."

"Did you see anyone else on the premises?" Davis asked,

"No, I met an old hayseed in a pickup truck as I was leaving but saw no one else."

"You mentioned earlier that someone took a shot at you. Tell me about that," Charley requested.

"It was the day before you barged into my room. I was on my way to Cartersville to get something to eat and maybe a couple of drinks. Not knowing the area, I turned off the highway an exit or two sooner than I should've. Earlier, I noticed a tan colored vehicle behind me, but paid little attention to it until I got off the interstate and saw he was still behind me."

"You said he, are you sure it was a man.?" Davis asked.

"It was definitely a man. He had on a Halloween mask of some kind. I was too busy dodging to get a good look at him, but it was a man. He shot at me when he went past. He then turned around and came back at me," Greenleaf explained.

The three men talked for a few more minutes. Davis pulled a small Bible from his pocket when they were ready to leave. He held it up for Jon Greenleaf to see. "I'm going to deposit this with the jailer when I leave and ask him to give it to you. You're going to have to pass the time somehow, and I can think of no better way than by reading this," he told Greenleaf. The man that had been described as *THE COWARDLY LION*—the man, who one deputy sheriff labeled as a motor-mouth, stood silently with his mouth open as Davis and Charley left the room.

***

"I should get you home before your wife arrives, and she'll be none-the-wiser," Charley told Davis after they made their way to Interstate 75 for their return trip.

"You're making me feel guilty, as if I'm lying to my wife," Davis snapped at Charley.

"Well, aren't you? I once heard you say in a sermon that sometimes by withholding information, we're lying."

Davis was pondering how he could argue with his own words when he heard a siren. He looked back to see two patrol cars with lights flashing. One of the cars pulled directly behind them while the other sped past and moved into their lane to occupy the space just ahead of them. "I believe they want us to pull over," Charley said. He steered his own vehicle to the side of the payment. Four uniformed officers jumped out of the two marked cars

"Both of you, out of the car with your hands where I can see them," one of the officers bellowed.

CHAPTER 16

"**P**ut your hands on top of your car and spread your legs," the officer told them.

Davis and Charley did as they were told. The policeman doing the talking frisked Charley and then Davis.

"What's this all about?" Charley asked when they turned to face the two policemen. I'm Charley Nelson, an officer on the Adairsville force and this is Davis Morgan, our chaplain. With your permission, I'll reach into my pocket for my identification."

"Go ahead," the officer told him, while holding his revolver in his right hand. "And yours too," he nodded toward Davis. "I also need to see your identification." When he received them, he looked carefully at both pieces. "Where's your vehicle registration?" He looked toward Charley.

"It's in the glove compartment," Charley responded. "There's a gun in there. As a law enforcement officer, I, of course, am licensed."

One of the officers pulled out the registration and the gun. "Please stand over there," the cop giving the orders told them, pointing toward an area away from the highway.

Two of the policemen stood guard over them while the other two searched Charley's car.

One of the cops searching the car took the keys from the ignition to open the trunk. He removed a few items, including the spare tire. Then the officer hollered, "Here it is." He held up what looked like a small white brick. "It looks like cocaine," he bellowed.

Davis and Charley were handcuffed, read their Maranda rights, and put into the back of one of the Drug Task Force patrol cars to be taken back to the jail complex. "I guess your wife is going to find out about this trip after all," Charley said. Davis didn't find Charley's remark the least bit funny. "I hope you know me well enough to know this is a set up." Charley said to Davis just before they pulled into the parking lot of the jail.

"There's no doubt in my mind about that," Davis replied.

***

Two days after that horrible experience in Cartersville, it all seemed like one of those half-awake, half-asleep dreams that Davis sometimes has on nights when he's restless. He was kept at the jail complex for more than three hours answering a lot of ridiculous questions. Finally, the people in charge decided he must be an innocent party traveling with Charley. They found no evidence he had any tie to or knowledge of the drugs found in Charley's trunk. He was not booked and told to go home. Charley was booked for drug possession.

"Pick you up where?" Deidre asked when he telephoned for a ride home. Davis knew he had a lot of explaining to do when Deidre arrived. He decided the ride home wouldn't be pleasant for him and it wasn't. How do you explain to the wife you love that you are expected of drug violations?

Davis learned in the interviews he endured earlier that evening that an anonymous person telephoned the offices of the drug task force, giving the description and plate number of Charley's car. The informant dropped the information that it would be carrying a significant quantity of drugs up highway 75 that very evening.

When he got home, Davis first called Dean to inform him of Charley's status. Dean was stunned all most beyond words. He then contacted Chief Hanson who seemed to be shocked but revealed little sympathy for his young officer.

The judge knew Charley, and the policeman's record was spotless. Those factors probably contributed to the judge setting a relatively low bail. Dean provided the bail money, and it was Davis's understanding that Charley would be released sometime late this day. All this weighted heavy on Davis's mind as did the news he heard a few minutes earlier. The Rat-Face Man reportedly stole a car in central Kentucky. *He's headed in this direction. There's no doubt in my mind he's coming after me. With Charley suspended, I doubt we'll get much protection from the police department.*

***

Mrs. Edison left a half hour earlier. Janie wasn't sure where she had gone, but she was glad to be free for a few minutes of her mother's badgering. The doorbell rang. Janie opened the door to see two well-dressed people. A beautiful brunette lady who looked familiar stood beside a tall man with touches of grey in his hair. The man took his sun glasses off and smiled when he saw her. "Janie?" he asked.

"Yes, I'm Janie. Can I help you?"

"I'm Raymond Matthews. You might recognize this young lady," he said turning his head toward the brunette beside him. "She is Caroline Robertson. I'm her agent and attorney. Can we come in for a few moments please?"

"Sure," she said stepping out of their way, still confused about who exactly they were. "Come on in and find a seat."

"We are here to apologize, aren't we Caroline?" He paused and looked at his client.

"Yes, that's right," the girl said without looking toward Janie.

Caroline Robertson, that's Devan's fiancée. She's the one who ran me off the road. That's why she looks familiar. Now it was coming together for Janie.

"You may or may not know that Ms. Robertson was the person who caused you the trouble on the highway the other day. She wasn't herself that day, and she's genuinely sorry. She wants to tell you the whole story and beg for your forgiveness, don't you Caroline?" The agent looked sternly at his client.

"I guess so," Caroline responded after a brief silence.

"Tell her what happened," Mr. Matthews instructed Caroline.

Caroline Robertson began what obviously was a well-rehearsed story. "After attending Devan's funeral, I was totally distraught. I guess I needed to strike out at someone, and since I didn't know who murdered him, you were the one I choose. I got in my car and drove back here looking for you. After a few drinks, I followed you up the road. The plan was to scare you. There was no intention of seriously hurting you. That's why I selected a place where there was a level plowed field to run you off the road. I don't know what got into me. I'm normally not that kind of person, and I'm truly sorry."

"We know this is a serious matter. We don't take it lightly, but we really would like to avoid any legal problems. I have here a check that Ms. Robertson has written, made out to you. It should cover any damages to your car as well as giving you a few dollars for the inconvenience we've cost you."

Raymond Matthews handed Janie a check. The word that came to mind when she glanced at it was, wow! This was a good deal more money than her car could have been bought for when it was new.

"Will that cover it?" Matthews asked when he saw her looking at the draft.

"This is more than enough to cover the damages." Janie answered, "Ms. Robertson is very generous."

"Well, she's really not a bad person, and we wanted you to know that. If anything comes up concerning this matter, I want you to give me a call," Matthews said and handed a business card to the somewhat dazed Janie.

After they left, Janie picked up her phone and called Davis. "You'll never believe what just happened..."

***

Charley drove straight to Davis's house after being released from county jail. Davis and Deidre were preparing dinner when the doorbell rang. "Come on in," Davis directed the unshaven young man standing before him.

"Are you sure you want a jailbird in your home?" Charley asked him.

"We don't worry about a man's past here," Davis joked and then felt bad about what he said.

"We're getting dinner ready. Walk with me to the kitchen, and I'll get a couple more hamburgers to put on the grill. We would be thrilled to have you as our guest for dinner."

"Ordinarily, I wouldn't intrude, but that jail food was terrible. A nice big hamburger sounds great."

When they went into the kitchen, Deidre embraced Charley, "I'm sorry for everything you've had to go through these last two or three days. Sometimes life just isn't fair," she sympathized.

"Thanks for believing in me," Charley replied. "I was afraid everyone would assume I'm a drug addict or worse, a drug dealer and not have anything to do with me."

"We know better than that." Deidre smiled at him and put her hand on his shoulder.

"Do you have any idea about who's trying to frame you?" Davis asked while standing over the grill to flip the hamburgers.

"Whoever it is isn't just *trying*, he's doing it. The way things look right now, I may not only lose my badge, but I, very well, could do some time. And I don't have an idea who's behind it," Charley lamented.

"It's all going to come out in the wash," Davis assured him.

"I wish I had your confidence," Charley responded.

"Is there anyone who would do something like this to get even with you for busting them in the past, or maybe someone trying to obstruct something you're working on now?" Davis asked.

"I can't think of anyone with a grudge big enough to cause them to do something like this," Charley replied. "And as to it being someone trying to impede an investigation, I'm just an officer, not a detective."

"What about your personal life? Is there anyone with whom you have had a falling out lately?"

"No one. I can't think of one person, except maybe for Dean. We argue occasionally," Charley admitted with a grin.

"Maybe it's about this murder case we've been looking into," Davis suggested. "Perhaps we've made someone nervous with all the questions we've asked. Whoever planted that cocaine in your car might have thought they could take both of us out of circulation with their little trick."

"I've considered that, but it just doesn't seem likely to me," Charley submitted. "Of course, those movie types would, no doubt, know how to get their hands on the drugs."

"That's what I was thinking, but at this point, I have no clear suspect in mind. Don't worry Charley, at some point it's all going to fall together."

"I hope you're right. All I've ever wanted to do is be a policeman. This could bring that to an abrupt end. And, as for my someday being chief like my dad, the possibility of that dream becoming a reality may have already reached the zero mark."

"No, don't think that way. We'll get to the bottom of it, and your position on the Adairsville police force will be stronger than ever. You just wait and see." Davis assured him. "Incidentally, I heard a little while ago that the Rat-Face Man is suspected of stealing a car in central Kentucky. It sounds like he's headed this way."

"It doesn't surprise me," Charley reacted. "When was the car stolen?"

"I think earlier today," Davis answered.

"I don't think you need to worry about him being in this area until at least tomorrow. It sounds like they have a fairly good idea about his whereabouts. I wouldn't be surprised if he is caught before the night is over. If he's not caught by tomorrow, I'd like to hang around for a while until he's back behind bars. Any request I make to provide security for you will probably be ignored since I'm suspended. I'll call Jed. He's still a good friend. He'll keep an eye out for you while on duty."

"We'll be glad to have you." Davis responded. "I know what Garrett is capable of, and I worry about Deidre."

CHAPTER 17

Davis was glad to see Janie back at work when he arrived at the shop. "Is that a new outfit, Janie? I don't remember seeing it before. You're going to turn all the young men's heads today," he said. Then he remembered Devan and regretted his remarks. *Maybe it's too soon to tease her about turning heads,* he thought.

"I didn't think you ever saw any of my outfits. This is the first time I recall you commenting on one of them."

"I notice. I just need to do a better job of verbalizing my thoughts."

"In other words, you're saying you're not good about offering compliments," Janie summarized.

"That's about it. I'll try to do better in the future."

"I decided to use a few dollars of my recently attained wealth to get something new for myself," Janie explained.

"Good for you," Davis responded. "It does a girl good to be just a little bit extravagant once in a while."

"I'm not sure if you're calling me a spendthrift or telling me it's okay for me to spend more than I should for something I really don't need."

"I'm just trying to compliment you on looking really great today, but I seem to be failing miserably." Davis took off in the direction of his shop.

She's rebounding, Davis thought. *When she gets ornery, I know she's on her way back.*

Later in the morning, Davis called Chief Hanson to inquire about the status of Clive Garrett.

"I've heard nothing. As far as I know, he's still at large," the chief told him. "Don't worry though, they'll get him. It's seldom that any escapee runs around loose for more than a few days. He'll turn up, and they'll be on him like flees on a dog."

It's that word seldom that concerns me, Davis thought, *I would feel better if he used the word never. I can see Rat-Face being the one out of ten thousand who makes it.* He knew from his dealings with the man in the past that besides being a cold-blooded murderer, he was also resourceful and determined.

Tomorrow would be the last day of school with students before summer vacation. That was good since it would mean most of the time Deidre would be where he could keep an eye on her, but it also meant she would be home a lot, which is where Garrett is most likely to show up. Maybe he needed to suggest to her that she visit Amy and Jay in their restored country home six miles out of town. She would not only be away from the house, but she could be helpful to Amy for a few days.

Charley came by after lunch. He seemed distressed to get the news that Garrett had not yet been recaptured. "If he's coming after you, he could be here anytime now," Charley stated. "I suggest you stay with a crowd as much as possible. He's not likely to go after you in a crowd. Tonya and I want to take you and Deidre to dinner at the Adairsville Inn this evening. There are a couple of things we want to talk over with you, and dinner out will help keep you in a crowd."

"Sounds like a plan. We would love spending some time with the two of you."

Davis was pleased to see a middle-aged couple come into the shop. He left Charley sitting while he approached the man and woman asking, "May I help you find something?"

"We were told you might have some Eugenia Price books," the woman stated.

"I still have most of her novels. Many of them are signed copies. I'll show you where they are." Davis walked ahead of them to his Georgia authors and subjects section."

"We're primarily interested in her Florida series," the woman told him. "I think we have the rest of them."

"You're in luck. I have *Don Juan McQueen, Maria,* and *Margaret's Song* right here. In fact, you can have your choice of a signed or unsigned copy of *Don Juan McQueen,*" he told them.

"I'll be over here while you check them out. Let me know if you have questions."

It didn't take the couple long to decide. In three or four minutes they walked toward him with three books, including the signed one. "We'll take these three," they told him.

"Take them to Janie up front, and she'll take care of you. Thank you for coming in."

After the customers left, Davis told Charley, "You know, I've been thinking about it, and I've decided your problems and Devan's murder could very well be tied together. Possibly someone around here doesn't want you anywhere near that case. Planting those drugs would be a good way to keep you out of it. Even though we didn't know it, we may have been getting closer than we thought."

"Okay, that's possible. What else have you been thinking?" Charley asked.

"We were assuming that Devan's murder was somehow connected to his squabble with his sister over the family estate. Maybe it wasn't that at all. It could be his dating Janie. It happens, you know. Some old boyfriend can't deal with someone else moving in on his territory. Did you know your partner, Jed, once dated Janie for several months?

"Now that you mention it, I do remember that, but that must have been three years ago when they were barely out of their teens. Jed has been married for a couple of years," Charley pointed out. "You're not saying that Jed...?"

"I'm only making a point. I'm not accusing anyone," Davis responded.

Perhaps it's the other thing—the murder Devan witnessed fifteen years ago. I know it's a long shot, but what if the person who committed that murder were here and knew Devan could identify him?"

"That sounds farfetched, but I guess it's possible. We're only about a hundred miles from where that went down. The guilty party could be around here," Charley responded after thinking about it for a few seconds. "I suppose it would be pointless to ask you if you have any idea about the identity of the guilty party," Charley added.

"Too soon for that, but if we are on the right track, we'll figure it out sooner or later," Davis told him.

"I don't want to seem impatient, but I hope it's sooner rather than later. I don't enjoy walking around town with everyone glaring at me because they think I'm a drug dealer."

"Those who know you know best don't think that, and you've got a lot of friends in this town who believe in you," Davis assured him.

***

Davis and Deidre met Charley and Tonya at the restaurant at six o'clock. They were escorted to a table where their order was taken by a perky young waitress. "When will you be leaving for Jacksonville?" Deidre asked Tonya.

"My plans have been altered slightly," she answered. "When we thought Charley would be making the trip with me, we were planning to leave either late tomorrow evening or early Saturday morning. Because of his current legal problems, he can't leave the state. After rethinking my schedule, I plan to leave early Sunday afternoon," Tonya revealed.

"There's a good reason she's waiting until then," Charley offered. "We wanted to be in church together on Sunday."

"I'm glad to hear that. Is there a particular reason you want to be there this Sunday?" Davis asked.

"Yes, there is. You've been patient with me. You've tactfully taught and encouraged me for two years. Tonya and I have talked about it a lot for maybe two months. You've told me more than once that when my faith in Jesus is sufficient to cause me to turn from my sins, I need to confess Jesus and then be baptized. Tonya and I both feel as if we are ready. We want what you and Deidre have found. We're ready to give our lives to Jesus. I guess I've been waiting until I got myself totally straightened out before I took that step, but there have been some things come up recently that helped me understand I will never be able to do that on my own strength. I remember you once told me I needed simply to turn it over to Jesus, and then, with his power available to me, I could start to become the person he wants me to be. We don't want to wait any longer. Tonya and I are ready to embrace the Jesus you've so lovingly revealed to us. We want to be baptized on Sunday, and we want you to do the honors," Charley told him.

Davis was, at first, speechless. He was choked up, with tears starting to form in his eyes. Deidre reached down to take hold of his right hand and squeezed it. "I've been waiting for two years to hear those words," he declared. "And now that I've heard them, they're sweeter than I could have imagined. The two of you have made the most important decision you'll ever make in this life. Could we join hands and thank the Lord for what He's doing?" It must have looked strange to the others in the dining room when the four of them joined hands and Davis began his prayer, but to the four participants, it felt very natural. After the prayer, there was a lot of chatter coming from their table. It seemed that they all wanted to talk at the same time.

"You'll remember that I said there were a couple of things we wanted to tell you. I don't think I can hold off on the second item any longer." Charley submitted shortly after their food was delivered. "Tonya, do you want to tell them?" They looked at each other dreamy eyed before Charley placed his hand on top of Tonya's.

"Charley asked me to marry him, and I said yes," Tonya informed them.

"Congratulations!" Davis reached across the table to vigorously shake the hand of his friend. I knew if you looked hard enough for long enough, you'd eventually find that one who would agree to put up with you. The truth is, I've been praying about this for several months. I think she's the perfect match for you, the one who will, no doubt, make you happy."

"When's this going to happen?" Deidre asked.

"We haven't worked all that out yet." Charley told them. "There's this matter in Jacksonville that's got to be resolved and, who knows, maybe even a prison sentence to serve before we can finalize all our plans. But we both know what we want and are willing to wait if we must. Davis, we want you to conduct the service when the time comes." Charley added.

"And I want you to be my matron of honor," Tonya informed Deidre.

The party of four left the restaurant a happy group. "I'll take Tonya home and then come back to your house. I'm going to spend the night in my car on that little knoll beside your place. If Garrett comes, he's likely to come at night, and he'll think my car is just another parked vehicle that belongs there," Charley suggested. "Of course, being on suspension, I don't have a gun, but I have a telephone. With the station close enough to be seen, I can have the guys there in moments should he show up."

"I feel bad about you sitting outside in your car. Maybe it would be better for you to come in and sleep in our guest room or at least on the sofa," Davis told him.

"No, I can do more good by staying outside. The car you hear driving into the spot next door in about an hour will be mine,"

Charley told them before he and Tonya got into the car to drive away.

After parking the jeep and walking across their porch, Davis was ready to put the key in the lock to open the door when he noticed through the window panes in the door, light coming from the kitchen in the back of the house. "Honey, did we turn off all the lights when we left?"

"I'm sure we did," Deidre answered.

"I see a light coming from the kitchen." Davis opened the front door and slowly walked on his tip toes, down the hallway toward the closed kitchen door, trying to keep the wood floors of the old house from squeaking. "Be careful," Deidre whispered. She was so close behind him that at one point he thought he could feel her breath on his neck. Davis quietly opened a closet door and took out his baseball bat. He used it once to capture Garrett. Maybe lightening can strike twice. He paused before opening the kitchen door. Then he quickly pulled it open.

CHAPTER 18

Amy, who was reaching into the fridge when the kitchen door suddenly opened, sharply turned her head in the direction of the sound. She saw her dad standing in the doorway with his baseball bat in hand. "Please don't hurt me! If I'd known your ice cream and pickles meant so much to you, I would've resisted the cravings and stayed away from your refrigerator," she said with a sparkle in her eyes.

After they all had a big laugh over the incident, they moved into the living room. Amy, carrying a small bowl of vanilla ice cream with a quarter of a dill pickle on the side, explained her presence. "Jay went to the church for men's chorus practice. I didn't want to sit in a pew while they went over the same songs again and again, so I insisted he drop me off here."

"We're just glad it was you and not the Rat-Face Man," Davis explained.

"You should be able to distinguish a rat from an elephant," Amy remarked with a giggle while patting her ample belly with her left hand. "Where have you guys been?" she asked. "Somewhere fun I hope."

"It was a fun evening all right," Davis responded. "We went to dinner with Charley and Tonya at the Inn."

"Seems like those two are getting sort of serious. Have they set a date yet?" Amy asked.

"Stay tuned," Deidre suggested. "If all goes well, there should be an announcement soon."

"In the meantime, there's something even more important coming up for them." Davis told her.

"What could be more important than matrimony?" Amy questioned.

"Be sure to be in church on Sunday," Davis urged.

"You don't mean to say that Charley has finally made a decision to accept the Lord?" Amy asked.

"Not only Charley, but Tonya as well. They both are planning to be baptized this Lord's day," Davis reported.

"That news is worth the six-mile trip in from Folsom. I know you've been working with and praying for Charley for a long time. This must mean a lot to you."

"It means a young man, whom I love like a brother, will be in Heaven someday. Yes, it means a lot to me!" Davis admitted.

A few minutes later, Davis heard what he assumed was Charley's car drive into the space next door. He got up and went to the window to make sure. It was indeed his friend's vehicle. He immediately felt safer. Shortly afterwards, Jay stopped by to retrieve his wife. "You can take that jar of pickles with you if you like, but I want to keep my ice cream." Davis chuckled.

"We're well stocked with pickles," Jay told him. "You can keep your pickles too."

Davis and Deidre talked for a few minutes. "Being the last day of school, tomorrow is a big day. I think I'm going to bed and read my Dani Pettrey book for a few minutes. Probably won't take me long to fall asleep," Deidre predicted.

"I think I'm too excited to sleep. I'm going to turn the TV on and see if any of the Brave's game is left. I'll be in after a while." There were a couple of innings of the game still to play, but despite being a devoted baseball fan, he comprehended little of what was happening on the screen. His mind was filled with happy thoughts of Charley and Tonya plus thoughts of another kind which featured a man who looked like a rat. Davis pondered everything he knew about Devan's murder and Charley's being framed. Rolling that information over in his mind, he was starting to form some possible conclusions that he didn't like. He tried his best to reject those thoughts, but they persisted.

***

Clive Garrett felt a little nervous about being in the medium-sized city of Chattanooga, Tennessee, just a few miles from the Georgia line. He knew he could be to Adairsville in an hour if he drove on interstate 75, but he also understood that the back roads, though they took longer, would be safer for him. He needed a gun, perhaps a rifle and a pistol. It was less than a half hour till midnight. He didn't like this second car he had stolen as much as the one he managed to get hold of in Kentucky, but to stay in the same car for the whole trip would be risky. He had to find a gun shop or some store that carried guns, and he needed to do so quickly. He would draw too much attention to himself by being on the streets after the midnight hour.

If I don't find a gun shop or a sporting goods store that carries guns, I can always find what I need in a farm house somewhere between here and Adairsville. All these people down here own guns, and it shouldn't be hard to relieve someone of at least one of those weapons. I'll find a way to get Morgan. No one has ever treated me the way he did. I told him he was a dead man, and I'm a man of my word. Then it's on to Miami and out of the country, he told himself.

Clive was still amazed they pulled off the escape. He and Fred, his partner in the getaway, went in opposite directions shortly after getting free. Fred went north to Canada and him south to Adairsville and ultimately to Miami. He had friends there who would help get him out of the country. He wondered if Fred had made it to Canada yet. Nothing he heard on the car radio indicated he'd been caught.

A police cruiser coming toward him caused Clive to hold his breath for an instant. With no gun, he was a dead duck if made by one of the coppers. He watched the car in his rear-view window until it was out of sight. He then turned his vehicle left just in case they turned around   and came back. *Too crowded here—too much to watch. I've got to find my way south and out of here. I'll get the weapon I need before sunrise. That's not going to be a problem.*

***

While Deidre was making pancakes and turkey bacon, Davis went out to Charley's car to invite him in for breakfast.

"I appreciate the invitation, but I thought I would join Dean and the fellas at the Little Rock this morning. I think I need to start fixing my image, and maybe breakfast with those guys would be a good place to begin," Charley told him. "You should be okay in the light of day. I'll be back before dark."

"That's not a bad idea, although I don't think you need to worry too much about your image. It hasn't been tarnished at all among those of us who know you," Davis responded.

"It's those that don't know me well that I worry about."

"Well, don't. I've got a feeling this thing is going to be resolved soon," Davis told him.

"Are you on to something?" Charley inquired.

"Not exactly," Davis replied. He wanted to encourage Charley, but not give him false hope. "I've got some ideas but need to make sure they pan out before making any accusations. It's sort of a puzzle that must be put together, and I'm not yet sure the pieces fit."

"I know you don't like to talk about these things until you're sure, but remember, I'm one of the victims this time. I'd be interested in hearing what you're thinking as soon as you feel free to share it with me," Charley urged his friend. He knew Davis had an uncanny knack for putting obscure facts together to come up with the right answers.

"You'll be the first to know when or if I come up with something more concrete. Enjoy your breakfast and don't let the guys get to you. They can be vicious with their horseplay. Don't pay a lot of attention to what they say," Davis told him.

"I'm disappointed," Deidre said when she learned Charley would not share their breakfast. "I've made all these pancakes, and now some of them will go to waste."

"No, they won't go to waste. I do enjoy good pancakes," Davis told her. "And I can use the turkey bacon that is left over to make a BLT for lunch."

"That's fine," she told her husband, but you would do well to remember what your cardiologist told you about your weight."

Davis did not reply to Deidre's word of caution. "I've been thinking," he said before pausing for an instant. "With this being the last day of school before summer vacation, it would be a good time for you to visit with Amy and Jay for a couple of days. With the baby only a little over a month away, I'm sure Amy could use the help."

"Amy's a big girl and even though she's pregnant, she can take care of herself. You're not fooling me for a moment, Davis Morgan. You're trying to get me away from this house because you think that escaped convict might show up. The only time we have been separated since we were married was the time you spent in the hospital with your heart attack. And, even though I wasn't in the room with you then, I was nearby. You can't get rid of me that easy." She then quoted Ruth 1:16 which Davis recognized as Ruth's commitment to her mother-in-law, Naomi, *Don't urge me to leave you or turn back from you. Where you go I will go, and where you stay I will stay. Your people will be my people and your God my God...*

"You've got that one down pat," Davis said with a slight chuckle. "But do you remember the next verse, *"Where you die I will die, and there I will be buried..."*

"Even if Garrett is after me, I suspect he will be caught before he gets anywhere near us," Davis told her.

"Is that why Charley spent the night in his car last night?" She asked.

"We're just being cautious," Davis assured her. "The chances of his getting to us, even if he is trying, are very slim."

"Well, if he does beat the odds and shows up, I'm going to be right here with you. I'm rapidly learning there is no problem we together cannot handle with the help of the Lord," she assured him.

"How can I argue with that?" Davis responded. He helped Deidre clean up the kitchen and kissed her before she left the house. "Have a great last day of school," he told her. He stood at the door, and with an uneasy feeling, watched her get into her car. He believed what she said about the two of them together with Jesus handling life's problems, but there was a lot he did not understand that sometimes bothered him. Even though he had seminary training and spent twenty-five years in the ministry, he believed that between the two of them, Deidre's faith far exceeded his own.

CHAPTER 19

The day went slowly for Deidre. The last day of school always did. Seniors graduated earlier in the week. All tests were completed, and this was basically a day set aside to complete state requirements for classroom time. If their behavior warranted it, Deidre allowed her students more flexibility than usual. It had been a good year—her first as Mrs. Morgan. She remembered the thrill she felt when students first started calling her that. There was time away from the classroom in the middle of the school year when Davis was recovering from his heart attack, but since that overlapped with Christmas vacation, she didn't lose an exorbitant amount of time.

Life was even more special for her since then. She wasn't sure exactly why, except maybe she felt every day she had with her husband since then was bonus time. She was looking forward to summer vacation and the things they were planning for the two and one-half months that would be available to them. She especially was anticipating a two-week trip to Cape Cod. She got a taste of the cape when they were there for their brief honeymoon, and now she was living for the day when she would be walking the beaches with her husband. The various theater productions and concerts would also be to her liking. As a history teacher, she loved the oldness of that area and couldn't wait to explore it.

Other matters kept trying to crowd out the pleasant summer plans. She was concerned about the charges of drug possession against Charley. She kept seeing a picture in her mind of a man with a face like a rat wearing prison garb. Janie, and her recent loss was another unpleasant thought that Deidre couldn't eliminate from her mind. *I guess there will always be problems right along with the blessings,* she almost spoke out loud before catching herself. *Such is life.*

Deidre gleefully pondered how far her relationship with Davis had come. It was his maturity and his gentlemanly nature that first drew her to him. But, like her, he had some real issues in those days. She wondered in those early months if he would ever be able to love anyone else after losing Julie. He didn't seem capable of committing to another. With Julie gone, Davis doted on Amy to the extent that he couldn't accept anyone who showed any interest in her. Along with those conflicts was the guilt he experienced about leaving the ministry, feeling he was not capable of continuing in the work he had done for all most twenty-five years. As he himself told her in more recent days, he was a mess. All that, however, was behind him, and their life together was nothing short of wonderful. Thinking about her husband, Deidre couldn't wait to get home. They would eat dinner together in their living room. She would make that salad he liked so much. There would be a lot of laugher, and they would talk about their plans for the summer. It would be a special evening in every way. She would make sure of that.

***

It was mid-afternoon when Chief Hanson dropped by the bookshop with a serious look on his face. "I thought you would want to know. The pawn shop on the corner of highway 140 and North Main was broken into last night or before daybreak this morning. Several guns were stolen along with a supply of ammunition. I doubt it was Garrett. I personally don't think there is any way he could've traveled this far without getting caught. However, just in case, I wanted you to know. We'll beef up our patrol around your place," He told a stunned Davis.

It's him. There's no doubt in my mind that he is here in Adairsville. "I thought when I saw you coming that you were bringing me some good news, like maybe he'd been recaptured," Davis suggested.

"I wish that were the case," Hanson responded. "But no such luck. I don't know how he has managed to elude the authorities for this long. Every law enforcement officer on the Eastern side of the country is on the lookout for him and his partner."

"I appreciate you letting me know about the break-in. I'll watch my back." Since you're here, there is something else I want to talk with you about. Maybe I'm out of order and need to mind my own business, but I'm going to tell you anyway that Charley is mighty discouraged by your attitude toward him since that drug bust. I know you had no choice but to suspend him. He knows that too, and that's not what bothers him. It's that he hasn't received the support from you that he thought he would get," Davis told Chief Hanson. "I think he feels the boys down at Cartersville might be a little more inclined to look into the possibility of a frame if they were convinced you thought him innocent."

"The problem with that is that I'm not fully convinced he is innocent," the chief replied.

"It's true that Charley's been a good cop these last four years. I guess you could say for the last year he has been my right-hand man, but that doesn't mean he can't make some terrible mistakes. I've seen it happen before. In a weak moment, a good man does something he shouldn't do. He may regret it latter, but that doesn't mean we can overlook the fact that he broke the law."

"Charley loves being a cop. I don't think he would jeopardize his position on the force by doing something stupid like what he's been accused of. I happen to know Charley well, and I know how he hates drugs and their disastrous effect on young people," Davis argued.

"The fact is a neighbor of Charley's told me that two or three days before the drugs were discovered in Charley's car, he saw him stumbling and falling all over his front yard, as if he were on something. It all ties together," the chief insisted.

"I know about that, and I know it was alcohol, not drugs that had him in that condition. I'm not defending him for that, but it was a personal problem that triggered that indiscretion. Prior to that, he had not taken even one drink for several months," Davis explained.

"If he was driven to alcohol by a personal problem, he could just as well have turned to cocaine." Hanson contended.

"You can believe whatever you wish, but I know Charley's not guilty, and I'll do everything I can to prove it," Davis told the chief.

"You'd best stay out of it. Remember, you were in that car too. You're lucky you weren't charged, but that could change, you know," Hanson warned before turning to leave the shop.

***

School was out not only for the day, but for the summer. Amy was elated. Now, if she could only deliver this baby and find some relief from the discomfort she was experiencing, life would be good again. Amy used the rearview mirror to keep her eye on the car behind her. She had not forgotten that it was a ploy with an approaching car that the Rat-Face Man and his partner used to kidnap her and put her through the most terrifying time of her life. She was relieved when she saw the car behind her turn to the right. She would be home in five minutes and, for a reason she didn't really understand, she felt safe there.

She didn't think much about it, when her dad first told her about Garrett's escape from prison. She figured they would pick him up in a day or two and the crisis would be over, but now several days had passed, and it was even possible that he could be in their area again, stalking them as he had done before. This time it would be his own need for revenge that drove him, and Amy concluded that made him even more dangerous.

She tried to put up a good front for her dad and her husband, but the truth was she was becoming more and more afraid with each passing day. She was more concerned for her father than for herself. It was him who had been threatened, but she suspected that if the man got the opportunity to harm her, he would not hesitate.

It's ironic, Amy thought. *The last time we had to deal with Rat-Face, it was just before my wedding, and here he is again just before I have my first child. Is this man going to show up before every important event in my life to torment me?*

Amy drove into her driveway and sat for a moment to admire the beautiful old farm house Jay had done such a great job restoring. She could see Ace and Buck in the pasture to the east of the house. She loved having horses and looked forward to the time when she could again ride. She hoped her soon-to-be-born baby boy would grow to love horses as much as she does. Jay had never been around horses or any kind of farm animals before they were married, but through her influence, his appreciation for them was coming along nicely. He was becoming quite the horseman.

Amy got out of her car and looked around to make sure no one was disturbing her little haven. When she got inside she locked the door behind her and walked through the house to the back door to make sure it was locked. Jay would be home in less than two hours and all would be well.

***

Clive Garrett was able to get the vehicle he was driving to a place on Boyd mountain that he remembered from his last visit to Adairsville. It was a logging road that obviously had not been used for that purpose in several years. He had food, water, guns, and ammunition. That's all he needed now for survival and to do the job he was there to do. He would remain here, resting until early morning. Then, before daylight, he would travel down to old town Adairsville where Morgan lived and get the job done.

Having not pulled a trigger for around two years, he wished he could shoot a few practice rounds before darkness set in. He had plenty of ammunition to enable him to do that, but he dared not use it. Someone might hear his shots and come to investigate. He knew it would not be wise to draw any kind of attention to himself, but it really didn't matter. He had always been an exceptional shot, and he was sure that had not changed. He hoped Morgan still lived in the house beside the railroad tracts. It didn't matter. Wherever he lived, he would find and snuff him.

Garrett had a pistol lying on the front seat, along with two rifles with stocks on the floor board and barrels propped on the edge of the seat pointed away from him. He had two more rifles and another pistol in the back seat.

I was lucky to spot that pawn shop. I don't remember it being there when I was here before. What a great selection of weapons and plenty of ammunition. Everything's going my way. Morgan has no chance whatsoever. Garrett found the release at his side and lowered the back of his seat. He locked the doors and laid back to get the sleep he missed the last two days. He wanted to be fresh for the job he had to do. With guns an arm length away, he had no reservations about closing his eyes to get the rest he needed.

CHAPTER 20

When Davis awakened on Saturday morning, he propped on his right arm. For fifteen minutes or more he watched his wife sleeping next to him. Finally, she stirred and opened her eyes to see him focused on her. "What're you staring at?" she asked. "Is there a smudge or something on my face?"

"I'm looking at the most beautiful woman in the world. You're amazing, and I can't believe you're my wife," Davis responded.

"You're full of malarkey but go ahead. I like it anyhow," Deidre told him, giggling. "What has you in such a delightful mood this morning?"

"I think it's suddenly waking up to realize I'm a man blessed far beyond anything I deserve. Thank you for the wonderful evening. Thank you for being my wife."

A few minutes later, Davis, as he had done the previous morning, went out to Charley's vehicle to invite him to breakfast. This time he accepted. "Not much happens in this part of town after midnight," he told them as they ate. "A car occasionally passes, but not very often. I think I saw less than ten cars between one o'clock and five-thirty. Almost as many trains as cars," Charley added. "Don't those trains keep you awake?" he asked.

"Not at all," Davis replied. "With them going by regularly, you get accustomed to it and ultimately don't even notice the noise. It's just part of the normal background track. It's like the soundtrack of a movie. Unless it's exceptional, we often don't even notice there is any music."

"It's hard for me to believe anything happens around you that you don't notice. I used to think you were ahead of most of us in solving these cases because you were so much smarter than us. Recently, I realized it's not that you are super intelligent that enables you to come up with the answers. You're not smarter than the rest of us, but you're more observant. You see and hear things most of us miss," Charley suggested.

"Thank you, Charley—I think. If I have such an ability, it's not a gift, but rather, a natural outgrowth of my early introverted personality. Until I became a pastor and was forced out of that mold, I observed and listened instead of talking. My college roommate used to tell people, 'My roommate doesn't talk much, but he sees everything that goes on.'"

"What about my case?" Have you seen or heard anything that might help us find the person who put that cocaine in my car?" Charley asked with a pleading tone to his voice.

"As, I am sure you know, Charley, it's usually not a matter of coming up with one fact or bit of evidence. It's most often a series of things that point toward one person that leads us to him. I think I see such a pattern emerging in your case and if it pans out, we'll talk about it in the next couple of days."

"We could talk about it now," Charley remarked.

"We could, but I don't want to accuse anyone until I'm relatively sure. I know you're anxious to get rid of this thing hanging over your head but be patient. It's going to work out," Davis told him.

"You keep saying that, but so far, I've seen no progress. I'm just as close to a drug conviction as I was two or three days ago. My life is a mess. I just want it all to go away."

"It will Charley," Davis assured him. "Don't worry. Just give it a little time."

There was mostly silence for the next few minutes. Davis's heart ached for Charley. *He's always been a good friend, and he doesn't deserve this. Lord, help him find some peace of mind...*

***

The Rat-Face Man was back on Boyd Mountain with his car parked on the same logging road as before. He had taken an early morning ride to old town Adairsville only to come back disappointed. When he drove past the place where he assumed Morgan still lived, he spotted a car parked near the house with someone, no doubt a body guard, sunk low in the driver's seat. Evidently, they were expecting him, but that wouldn't stop him. He could easily have blown the guard away, but the shot might very well have drawn someone else there before he could get to his real target. It would require a little planning. He would have to find Morgan in an isolated spot. He had waited this long, he could wait a little longer.

Garrett decided to stretch his legs. He took a rifle, put a pistol in his belt and made sure he had plenty of ammo before locking the car. He walked approximately a quarter of a mile on what had once been a road capable of supporting trucks with loads of logs, but now, due to little or no use, there were slightly washed out grooves where the tires had once rolled. Weeds and small bushes were threatening to take over. It was little more than a trail. Garrett stayed on the road, not wanting to get into the growth on either side. He remembered that this part of the country was home to a lot of big snakes, and he didn't like snakes big or small.

Suddenly, Garrett heard voices up ahead. *I guess I don't have a choice. I'm going to have to get into the bushes despite the snakes.* He was careful where he put his feet, constantly looking at the ground as he headed for the high spot that would allow him to see who was in his woods. When he reached the knoll, he could see three boys in the distance, maybe thirteen or fourteen years old with packs on their backs. They were laughing and playing as they crossed the road headed down the mountain. Going in that direction, he wouldn't have to worry about them. They wouldn't spot him or his car. He was glad. He wouldn't feel good about blowing away boys that age. He would do it if he had to, but he wouldn't feel good about it.

When Garrett returned to his car, he found a place where he wouldn't expect to find snakes and sat on the ground leaning against a tree large enough to support his back. He needed to give some thought to how he'd go about terminating Morgan. He needed to come up with a plan. He remembered from his previous encounters with the man that he seemed to be the luckiest guy alive. Lucky or not, he'd get him this time.

***

On the spur of the moment, after Charley left, Davis and Deidre decided to use the day for some fun activities which they could do close to home. When Deidre suggested, Davis remembered Charley's warning about staying with large groups of people. He rationalized that apart from driving from venue to venue, they would, for the most part, be with other people. He said nothing to his wife about Charley's warning. They left the house, each dressed in baseball cap, jeans, and sneakers, ready to enjoy what was a beautiful day.

Their first stop was the strawberry patch near the neighboring town of Calhoun where numerous people were already busy picking their own strawberries. Both worked the field, picking the best berries they could find. They paid the farmer and left the patch with six small baskets of strawberries. "I don't know what we'll do with all these berries," Deidre remarked.

"I do," Davis responded. "I've always loved strawberries. When I was a child I used to eat them until I got a stomach ache. Maybe, if I don't eat them all, you could make some strawberry jam," Davis remarked after thinking about it for a moment.

"Sure, I can do that, and you can build that garage we talk about from time to time," Deidre remarked.

Their next stop was in front of the old company store in the little mill village of Shannon where several truck farmers often gather on Saturdays with their fruits and veggies. They purchased their first watermelon of the year, several ears of corn, a basket of tomatoes, and some peaches. "I love corn on the cob," Deidre commented.

From there, it was on to Rome and Dogwood Books, a rare and used bookshop that had long been one of Davis's favorite places. "Where is Kenneth today?" Davis asked the man behind the checkout counter. Kenneth was the owner and a longtime friend of Davis's.

"He decided to take the day off for some family time," the clerk explained.

"I don't blame him for that. It's a great day to be out and about," Davis told him. "I guess it's not fair to tell that to someone whose stuck inside."

"What can you do? Somebody has to mind the store." The clerk smiled.

Davis couldn't get out of the store without purchasing an Easton Press leather-bound copy of Charles *Dickens Great Expectations*. It had always been one of his favorite books, and he would have every Easton Press Classic ever published if he could afford them. Even with the standard discount he received from Kenneth, this one made a good-sized dent in his billfold.

"Just what you needed, another book," Deidre told him. "But I guess I ought to count my blessings. We got out of the store today spending a good deal less than usual."

"You know I've always subscribed to that old cliché, 'Buy books, and if you have any money left, buy food,'" Davis explained.

"I know. That's why I insisted we first go to the strawberry patch and farmer's market," Deidre remarked before she smiled. "I'm glad you got that beautiful copy of *Great Expectations*. It's one of my favorite books too, and it'll look great on the shelf with our other leather-bound classics."

After leaving the bookstore, Davis and Deidre drove to Panera for a late lunch. On the trip back to Adairsville, Deidre told her husband, "There's one more thing I would like to do before we return home. I'd like to go out to Jay and Amy's and work on my horseback riding skills."

"I'm game if you are," he told her. Neither of them had done a lot of riding before Amy got her horses, but it was an activity they were learning to enjoy. Charley's warning crossed Davis's mind. They would not be in a crowd of people there, but he decided it should be okay. He would keep a careful lookout. They couldn't quit living their lives because Garrett had escaped from prison.

Jay walked with them to the little barn where he helped them saddle up. Deidre mounted Ace, the smaller of the two animals. Buck was not only larger but friskier as well. Davis rode him. He was sure Deidre was a better rider than he, but he was stronger than her and felt the extra strength was sometimes required to handle Buck. They rode the back-property line before getting to a little used gravel road on which they meandered for a while. Deidre noticed Davis constantly looking to the left and right and occasionally glancing back while they rode, and she suddenly realized why. She decided she should not have suggested they add this activity to their day. It may have put them in a dangerous situation. "Honey, don't you think we've had enough? Maybe we'd better head back toward the barn," she suggested.

"I don't believe it! I outlasted you today. I'm usually the one yelling about having enough," Davis remarked.

"It's been fun, but it's been a long day," she told him. Both Jay and Amy were waiting for them at the barn when they returned.

"Are you ready to take your turn?" Davis asked his daughter.

"If I took a turn, it would have to be on Buck," she told him. "I would break Ace down for sure."

"Later in the evening, when Charley arrived for evening guard duty, Davis insisted he sleep on their sofa, rather than keeping guard from his car. He wanted him alert for the big day at church. After putting up minor resistance, he agreed only after contacting Jed and asking him to keep a close look out on the house while patrolling that evening.

CHAPTER 21

Davis woke early on Sunday morning from a good night's sleep. Charley was already up and stirring about when he went into the living room. "We'll have breakfast ready in a few minutes. You should have plenty of time to get ready and pick up Tonya before church time," Davis told him.

"I think I'll run through Bojangles's window for a biscuit and coffee on my way back to the apartment," he told Davis.

"So, you like their cooking better than mine," Davis teased.

"Do you bake biscuits?" Charley asked. "Truthfully, I don't know much about your cooking. Bojangles has been my breakfast place for a while now and old habits die hard."

Davis and Deidre hurried through their Sunday morning routine and were at church for their adult Bible study by ten o'clock. When they walked into the worship center a few minutes before eleven, they spotted Charley and Tonya in a pew about half-way back. Tonya was smiling. Charley looked a little nervous. Davis was relieved to see them. He wasn't sure why. He had always found Charley to be a man of his word, but he also knew Satan would do everything possible to halt a decision such as the one this couple was making. He and Deidre sat beside their friends but allowed the young couple to remain closest to the aisle.

The service started with one of Davis's favorite songs, a song of praise entitled, As a Deer. Suddenly, Davis was overcome with emotion. This was the day he had prayed for and dreamed of for two years. Today his best friend would complete his obedience to the Lord. Charley would no longer be only his friend, but his brother as well. He thought of the title of the old spiritual, *O Happy Day.*

Clark's sermon was appropriate. It was based on the story of the conversion of the Ethiopian in Acts chapter 8. In keeping with the tradition of this church, a song was sung after the sermon when anyone who wished to do so had the opportunity to make the decision on their hearts. At the beginning of the second stanza of the song, Charley and Tonya, hand in hand, stepped into the aisle and moved toward the preacher who received them. The preacher aided the two of them in repeating their good confession and then prayed with them. He motioned for Davis to go to the dressing room with Charley. Deidre went to the allotted place on the opposite side to help Tonya prepare for her baptism.

The first few verses of Romans 6 were read to the congregation, and then a hymn was sung as the baptismal candidates along with Davis prepared to go down into the four feet of water. Davis was the first to get into the baptistry. He extended a hand to help Tonya into the water and then turned back in the other direction to lead Charley down the four steps. While Charley waited at one end of the baptistry, Davis faced the congregation while Tonya turned toward Charley with her right side to the congregation. Davis took both her hands in his left hand and put his right on the small of her back. "Tonya Willis, upon your confession of faith and the repentance that preceded that confession, I now baptize you in the name of the Father, the Son and the Holy Spirit for the remission of your sins," Davis lifted her hands to her nose and mouth and lowered her backward into the water before gently raising her to a standing position.

The process was repeated with Charley while Tonya stood at the other end of the baptistry. Rising out of the water to his feet, Charley's face was plastered with a huge smile. The three of them formed a small circle as they hugged in the center of the baptistry. The entire congregation broke into spontaneous applause. The whole service took no more than five or six minutes, but it was among the most satisfying minutes in Davis's life. A dream had just become a reality.

***

Knowing Tonya would need to begin her drive to Jacksonville right away, Deidre invited the couple to join them for a light lunch at home. They ate quickly. Afterwards Davis and Deidre went to sit on the front porch to give their guests some privacy in which to say goodbye. "I guess this is what it means to have mixed emotions," Deidre remarked. "I am enormously happy for Charley and Tonya, having just made the most important decisions of their lives. At the same time, I'm heartbroken for them that they will be separated for who knows how long, with the legal troubles Charley is facing."

"I understand and feel the same way, but love finds a way. Do you remember what it says in Ecclesiastes chapter 8, verse 6?" Davis asked.

"No, I've no idea what that verse says. You'll have to tell me about that one," Deidre informed him.

"It says, 'For there is a proper time and procedure for every matter...' God knows exactly what he's doing. Sometimes it's hard, but we must learn to trust his timing. There may be some important reason why there needs to be some space between Charley and Tonya for a while. If that is true, we may never know what that reason is, but God does."

"I know, but it just doesn't seem fair," Deidre groaned.

"I guess what's best for us doesn't always seem fair. If we could see into the future, we might understand and be more accepting of these things we don't seem able to change, but we can't see into the future, and, that being the case, we must trust God." Davis said.

"When Julie died, my attitude was, why did God do this to me and to Julie? I saw it as being totally unfair. Now after some time has passed, I understand that Julie is in a better place, and I am finally able to rejoice in that. Julie and I had a great life together that I cherish, but now you and I have a beautiful life together here in this spot I so love. I'm not ready to say God was responsible for Julie's death, so He set all that in place. I do know He could have allowed Julie to live. That being the case, I must believe He had a plan for her, and He has a plan for us. And God's plan is always right for all concerned. It's best for us, even when we don't understand, just to accept it and get on with life."

"I think I've heard some of your best sermons right here on this porch," Deidre told him before leaning over to kiss him on the cheek. At that moment, they heard the noise the screen door always makes when being closed.

"Thank you for your wonderful hospitality," Tonya told them. "I need to get on down the road. I'm not comfortable driving too fast with that U-Haul trailer behind me, and I do want to get to my brother's house before midnight."

"We're so proud of you," Deidre told her while embracing her tightly. "You be careful on the road and come back to us safely. We're going to miss you until you're settled back here where you belong."

"What she said," Davis uttered when he hugged her. "You're in our prayers," he assured her.

Davis and Deidre went inside while Charley walked Tonya to her car.

"Going back to the apartment to get some rest," they heard Charley's voice through the screen door five minutes later. "I'll be back and on guard duty before sundown."

Deidre sat down with a book. She was soon dosing. Davis was tempted to turn on the TV to check on the Braves game but decided for the sake of Deidre's unplanned nap not to do so. Besides that, he needed some time to sit quietly and let his mind work. He wondered where Garrett would be if he had made it to Adairsville and was the one who had stolen the guns from the pawn shop. He obviously would not be in one of the motels. That would surely lead to a quick arrest. *Garrett is smarter than that.* Davis recalled that Garrett had been lodged in the Boyd Mountain area when here before. He might be more familiar with that neighborhood than anywhere else in the region. There were plenty of places up there to hide a car one might live in for two or three days without being detected. Perhaps tomorrow, he would talk with Charley about them driving up that way to take a look. He would need to find a safe place for Deidre if they decided to do so. Knowing of what Rat-Face was capable, he would not leave her at home alone until the killer was caught.

There was another complication to which Davis needed to give some thought. Had the time come for him to share with Charley his suspicions about Devan's murderer and the person who had framed him? He wasn't sure. His suspicions, at this point, were based on less than strong evidence. He had never known this person to be less than a law-abiding citizen, yet he couldn't help but believe he had it tied down. He would be more comfortable sharing his hunch if he had, at least, a pinch of proof. He needed to think about it more before spilling his thoughts to Charley. He needed to pray about it. *The fact is, I hope I'm totally off base,* he decided.

***

Even before getting through Atlanta, Tonya, with tears in her eyes, was already mourning her decision to leave Adairsville. She almost talked herself into turning the car around and going home, but she was somehow able to keep her vehicle pointed south. She loved her brother and he desperately needed her help. On the other hand, was she being fair to the man she loved and intended to marry, especially considering his current problems? He needed her too, maybe more than her brother.

She had already decided she would give her brother and his daughters no more than six months of her life. Surely, he could work something out in that length of time. She had heard nothing in the past couple of weeks about any romantic progress with the lady he was dating. She certainly didn't want him to make the mistake of marrying her simply to give the girls a mother. A good marriage would require a more noble motive than that. Maybe if that didn't work out, he could, in six months, get on better ground financially. That would enable him to afford a suitable nanny who could give the girls more quality time. What was she thinking when she made this commitment?

Another hour of driving enabled Tonya to calm down, and start thinking more optimistically. *God will work it out*, she decided. *Pull yourself together, girl, you're going to have to be mom to three little girls who need you in the worst way. Be strong for them.* She was gaining on it—starting to be a little more upbeat about the challenge ahead. She would be all right by the time she arrived. *Lord, I'm going to need your help. I can't do this alone...*

CHAPTER 22

On Monday morning, Davis talked Deidre, along with Barbara, into a trip to a Cartersville museum with a group from the church. Deidre had little enthusiasm for the outing, but she agreed to go because she sensed Davis had something in mind but needed for her to be in a safe environment. It was true, they had been married for less than a year, but she had no difficulty reading him. When she and Barbara were ready to leave, Deidre embraced her husband and kissed him. "I love you. Whatever you're up to, be careful. I don't want to lose you," she pleaded.

Before Davis and Charley started their drive up Boyd Mountain, at Charley's insistence, they went through the drive-through window at Bojangles's for coffee.

Earlier in the morning, while Deidre was in the kitchen and he and Charley in the living room, Davis considered revealing to Charley his theory about the identity of Devan's murderer and why he had been framed by that same person. Davis could think of five reasons he held to his conclusion, but some of his deductions were weak. He still had doubts. He didn't want to implicate an innocent person, so he decided to say nothing.

As anxious as Charley was, there was still time. He hoped he was wrong about who he suspected, but his instincts told him otherwise. Perhaps before this day was over he would feel free to share his thoughts with Charley.

Davis, being friends with the residents, drove into the drive of the house on the top of what was called Boyd Mountain by the people of Adairsville. From there, one can get a pretty good view of the little town below. More of the community can be seen during the months when no leaves on the trees block the view, but it provides a beautiful picture even in the late spring. Davis wondered if anyone had ever painted the view from there. He could see the steeples of two of the churches. Some of the downtown stores were visible as was a part of the elementary school. The large oak trees shading the town provided a look of elegance. The store fronts and downtown houses, more than one hundred years old, gave it a nineteenth-century look. Perhaps it was because no people could be seen that it looked so peaceful. It occurred to Davis that most often it was people that spoiled the peacefulness of a place. They sat silently for a couple of minutes enjoying the view below. "Oh, how I love that little town," Davis remarked.

"Well, it's home. I don't know any other place like it," Charley commented between sips from his coffee cup.

Driving ahead, they saw a gentleman in front of what looked like a freshly painted white house doing yard work in the morning hours perhaps before the sun got high enough to make it uncomfortable. Davis pulled into the drive. He opened his door to speak to the man. "Hello sir, I'm Davis Morgan, and this is Charley Nelson."

"Yes, I knew Charley's dad. A good man and the best policeman we ever had," he volunteered.

"Everything you say is true, and Charley is following in his dad's footsteps," Davis responded. "We were wondering if you've seen any vehicles up this way the last three or four days that might have seemed a little strange? Maybe with an out-of-state license plate."

"Now that you mention it, I did see a car pass by two or three times with a Tennessee plate," he told them. "I just figured he was visiting someone out this way."

"You said he. Was there just a man in the car or did he have passengers?" Charley asked.

"It looked like to me that there was only a driver in the car."

"Did you get a look at him?" Davis asked. "Could you describe him?"

"I didn't pay much attention, but I do remember he appeared to be a mature man, not young, but at least middle age."

"Did you catch what kind of car he was driving?" Charley inquired.

"I don't know much about cars." the gentleman scratched his head. "I could probably tell you more about it, had it been a pick-up," he informed them. "I do remember it was sort of a silver color."

"One more question and we'll let you get back to your work. When was the last time you saw him?" Davis asked.

"I think it was late Saturday, Yeah, that's right, it was day before yesterday."

"We could be on to something," Charley said as they drove away.

"Maybe," Davis responded. "But what will we do if we find him? Neither of us has a weapon. I understand he took several guns and plenty of ammunition from the pawn shop. Sounds like a one-sided battle."

"I don't know," Charley answered. "We have him outnumbered, and I hope we are smarter than him. I guess we'll have to decide that when or if we find him. Let's check out some of these abandoned logging roads and cow trails."

They drove another half mile before turning right onto what was once a road, probably used for farm work. They traveled no more than two hundred yards before it petered out. Davis was glad they had chosen to drive the Jeep. Its high frame and four-wheel drive made it ideal for these kinds of roads or, perhaps more correctly, trails. They turned around to head back to the main road where they turned right. Before they got very far, they came upon another so-called road to the right.

"Look at that," Charley urged, pointing toward the side road. "It looks like someone might have recently driven down that road. See how the weeds and small bushes are bent as if a car might have driven over them."

"You've been watching too many cowboy movies," Davis told him. "Now you think you're a frontier scout."

"Just get this heap on that road and keep your eyes peeled. It's going to be important that we see him before he sees us," Charley suggested.

"Then maybe we ought to park and get out and walk," Davis advised. "If he's out here, he'll hear us coming if we're riding."

"As much as I hate to admit it, you're right. Why don't you pull over there and park behind those trees?" Charley suggested.

Davis did as he was instructed. While walking, Davis saw a large piece of a limb about three feet long lying on the ground. He picked it up, looked at it and decided it was still strong enough for use. He carried it with him because he felt more secure approaching the Rat-Face Man with something in hand.

"That stick isn't going to help you against his guns," Charley told him.

"Maybe not, but it's comforting to at least have a weapon of some kind, as inadequate as it might seem." Davis was nervous but saw little evidence that Charley was anything but cool and calm. He was glad Charley oversaw this maneuver. He had learned to have full confidence in the young policeman who had been his partner in several uncomfortable situations over the last couple of years.

As they walked, they continued to notice that weeds and bushes were bent, conceivably from being recently driven over by a vehicle. Charley picked up a package that once contained cigarettes that obviously had not yet been exposed to rain and weather. "Is Garrett a smoker?" Charley asked.

"I don't know," Davis answered. "My guess would be yes, but that would be only a guess."

After walking what seemed to Davis like at least another mile, but, was probably less than half that, they came to a spot where several pieces of trash lay on the ground. The paper scattered about looked mostly to be food wrappers. Charley noticed this seemed to be where whoever had driven on the little road had stopped. The bushes and weeds ahead had not been crushed by tires rolling over them. "If our man was here, he's gone now," Charley stated.

"It might be worth staking out this spot, I suppose some kids or someone with unknown intentions could've left these traces of life, but it could also have been Garrett," Davis suggested.

By the time they got back to the Jeep, Davis was worn out, but he wasn't about to admit that to Charley who seemed fresh enough for another long stroll. "Where to now?" Charley asked.

"Wherever we decide to go, we can take the Jeep from here," Davis told him.

They dropped in for lunch at Dukes because Charley liked the wings. A waitress showed a lot of interest in Charley, but, for the first time Davis could remember, Charley didn't return the attention. *He's growing up,* Davis decided. *He'll never know how proud I am of him.*

Davis's phone rang before they left the restaurant. He received the call before putting the phone back into his pocket. "Chief Hanson wants me to meet him at Spring Bank around three o'clock. He says he has some questions to ask me about the day we found Devan," he announced to Charley. "Do you want to go with me?"

"Wouldn't miss it for the world," Charley told him.

"Well, we've got a little time to spare. What do you want to do?" Davis asked.

"You may think this silly, but we have almost two hours and that's plenty of time for us to drive to Calhoun to that little jewelry store downtown. I'm not ready to buy, but I would like to look at their rings to at least get an idea about price. I've heard that even though it's a small store, they stock some beautiful stuff, and the price is right."

"Not silly at all. I'd love to go with you." Davis responded.

"I suppose Tonya arrived safely last night," Davis remarked while driving north.

"Yes, she called when she arrived and said she had no problems on the road."

Davis mostly listened to Charley talk about Tonya on the fifteen-minute drive to the Calhoun jewelry shop. *He's got it bad,* Davis decided. *Can't think about anything else.* They spent almost a half-hour in the little jewelry shop looking at rings with Charley occasionally asking the question, "How much is this one?"

They returned to Adairsville a few minutes ahead of schedule, which enabled them to briefly stop at the house before starting the short drive to Spring Bank.

***

After they left the house and turned right onto College Street, Charley looked across the small park to his left and thought he caught a glimpse of a silver vehicle on Park Street also going west. He said nothing to Davis. *It's probably nothing. There're lots of silver colored cars in the world. No reason to alarm Davis. We'll know when College intersects with Park at the bottom of the hill.* There was no car in sight, silver or otherwise, when they came to the intersection. Charley continued to glance back as they traveled down the Hall Station Road, but he saw nothing that resembled a silver-colored car. However, he knew that meant little. A professional hit man like Garrett would know how to keep hidden while tailing another vehicle.

Charley touched his right side at the waist and wished he had his service revolver. He felt naked and vulnerable without it. Chief Hanson would certainly have his weapon when they reached Spring Bank. That thought bolstered his confidence.

CHAPTER 23

C hief Hanson's car was the only one in the small parking lot when Davis parked his Jeep. That was not surprising since the beautiful spot called Spring Bank is largely undiscovered and receives few visitors. Hanson was nowhere in sight. "He's probably at the big Oak tree since that's where the body was found," Davis suggested. The two men could hear gun shots coming from the nearby shooting range operated by Barnsley Garden resort.

"That's probably the reason no one recalled hearing the shot when Devan was killed out here," Charley speculated. "Gun shots are a regular occurrence."

"There he is." Davis pointed at a figure in uniform in the distance pacing under the large tree. They hurried in that direction. "Chief Hanson, I hope you haven't been waiting long," Davis greeted him.

"No, I just got here. I didn't know you'd have Nelson with you, but I guess that's good."

"You said you have some questions for me, Chief. I'm ready to tell you anything you want to know," Davis declared. "Go ahead and interrogate me all you want."

At first there was silence as Chief Hanson shifted his weight and slightly shuffled his feet while looking at the ground. Finally, he looked up at Davis. "You know, don't you?" he uttered.

"Know what?" Davis asked.

"Don't play dumb with me. You know exactly what I'm talking about. I've seen the looks you've given me when you thought I wasn't looking. I've not been completely oblivious to your attitude toward me. It's part of the job. I read people pretty well. You've suspected me for a while. I doubt you have any real evidence, but I know you and your chum here well enough to know that in time you will, if I don't put a stop to it here and now." The policeman reached for his gun. He pulled it out of the holster and held it at his side. It was almost as if he couldn't bear to point the weapon toward the two men who had often been his able supporters in the past.

Davis looked at Charley who stood speechless with his face as white as Davis had ever seen it. *That answers one question,* Davis thought. *Charley had no idea his chief was the guilty party.*

"I'm curious. What tipped you off?" the chief asked.

"It wasn't one factor, but a combination of several," Davis answered. "Greenleaf spoke of seeing an Adairsville Police Department car leaving here before he arrived. He assumed the driver was patrolling this area. But an Adairsville policeman would not be doing that. It's under the jurisdiction of the county sheriff. That rang the bell loudly. I understood that an Adairsville policeman could've been here for some reason other than to kill Devan, but then I started connecting the dots."

"Such as what?" Hanson asked.

"Well, you mentioned to me that you inherited a family farm near Commerce which is only a few miles from where the murder Devan witnessed took place," Davis told him.

"I remember regretting that almost as soon as it came out of my mouth. That's the reason I really didn't want to be around you, Davis. I never knew what you would pick up on. What else?" the chief asked. "I don't think that alone would point you toward me."

"No. There were two or three other components to the picture I was seeing," Davis continued.

"I heard you tell a group of men standing in front of the 1902 Stock Exchange that your sport was racing. The man who committed the murder that Devan witnessed was obviously a serious race fan. Then I recalled that, according to Charley, you were adamant about questioning Greenleaf before Sheriff Wilson got hold of him. You needed to know if he could identify you as the person in the patrol car on the day of Devan's murder. That's why you took a shot at him earlier. You thought if he was caught, you might be a goner. The best way for you to eliminate that threat was to kill him. Then, when Charley caught him, you were horrified, but greatly relieved after questioning him. You discovered he couldn't tie you to the crime."

"You're right," Hanson told him. "But I lived in fear that at some point, the light bulb might come on in the head of that freak."

"That light bulb may yet come on," Davis told him. "Especially after we are found shot to death, having come here to meet you."

"Maybe, but I don't think he's that bright," Bob responded. "The report everyone will hear is that I found you dead when I arrived here."

"For me..." Davis spoke up, knowing the longer he could keep Hanson talking, the longer they would stay alive. "For me, the final factor was when I discovered you were the only person on the Adairsville police force old enough to have been the murderer fifteen years ago. There is no other officer on the force over forty years of age. If it was an Adairsville policeman who killed Devan because Devan recognized him as the murderer from years ago, it had to be you, since that killer was identified as being between forty and fifty years old at the time," Davis explained.

"You do have a mind for detective work. I hate what I'm going to have to do to both of you, but I don't have a choice. I don't know why I need to explain myself to you, but I think I do," Hanson told them, still holding his revolver at his side.

"I killed that man fifteen years ago while out of my mind drunk. I hardly remember anything about it. I was that way a lot in those days—as they say, at the bottom of the barrel. I went to the police academy as a young man, but the job I went to the academy to get fell through and forced me to work in a mill for not much more than minimum wage while helping Dad with the little farm he fiddled with after selling his saw mill and lumber business. I hated my life and spent a lot of time trying to drown it out. There was no doubt in my mind after I killed that man, I had to get away from there. If I didn't, prison would become my home for the rest of my life. My wife had some relatives here in Adairsville, so we moved here. Having gone to the police academy, it was no problem for me to get a position on the force here when one opened. I kept my nose clean, stayed away from the bottle, and, in time, there was an opening for chief. Being a good deal older than the other officers and having a good record in my six years of employment here, it was easy enough for me to get that position. The years that followed were good years—the best years of my life, I guess. I was liked and respected, and I loved it. I had almost forgotten what I did fifteen years ago. Then Rhodes came along and immediately recognized me."

"He was a parasite if there ever was one. He told me all I had to do was give him two hundred thousand dollars and no one would ever know I killed anyone. I don't have that kind of money. Oh, I could've cashed in my retirement and a life insurance policy to come up with a little more than half that amount. Maybe I could have, in time, sold the little farm in Commerce to get the rest of it, but that would take months, and he wanted it in two weeks. I figured if I did come up with the money to pay him, I would be shelling it out for the rest of my life."

"So, you killed him," Davis concluded.

"When I heard he was out here, I decided it would be a good, isolated place to confront him again and try to come to some other arrangement, but it didn't go well. I ended up losing my temper, pulling my gun and shooting him before I knew what I had done.

"And you're the person who planted the drugs in my car," Charley, who up to this point had remained silent, offered.

"I tried to discourage the two of you from getting involved. When you ignored me and went ahead with your meddling, I knew I had to stop you somehow. I thought the drugs were a good way to do that. I was a little disappointed when they sent you home, Davis. I thought both of you would end up in more trouble than you've ever seen before," Hanson told them.

"You don't really think you're going to get away with leaving us dead here on the ground, do you?" Davis asked. "Where does it all stop? You can't just keep shooting everyone who's a threat to you."

"I don't..."

All three men heard the noise at the same time. It was not very loud, maybe the sound of someone in the distance stepping on something like a stick. Hanson looked up and both Davis and Charley turned their heads in the direction from which the sound came. Davis was shocked at what he saw. It was Garrett, the Rat-Face Man. He was on one knee with a rifle aimed in their direction, ready to pull the trigger.

CHAPTER 24

It took Davis only a split second to conclude that Garrett would take his first shot at the man with the gun. He would first eliminate the only one who could hurt him. Instinctively, Davis jumped in front of Hanson, threw up both arms and cried, "No! No!"

The shot echoed. The impact of the bullet caused Davis to fly backwards into Chief Hanson before his limp body fell to the ground at the feet of the chief. The momentarily stunned Hanson raised his revolver, and pointed it toward the man with the rifle, but before he could fire, Garrett got off another shot, and the chief fell into a heap beside Davis.

Charley made a dash toward the gun the chief dropped when he was hit. Garrett fired a shot at the moving target, but this time missed. Charley picked up the pistol on the move and zig zagged as he ran toward the man with the rifle. When Garrett took a second shot at the quick moving young policeman running in his direction, Charley dove to the ground and fired the gun in his hand three times in the direction of the would-be assassin. At least two of the bullets found their mark and the Rat-Face Man fell to the ground.

Charley sprung to his feet and ran to the man he had just brought down. He took the rifle and flung it as far as he could. He pulled a revolver from the waist band of the bleeding man and pitched it away. In a matter of seconds, he had his phone out of his pocket, punched 911 and shouted into the phone, "This is officer Charley Nelson. I'm at Spring Bank near Kingston. Three men are down, and I need an ambulance now!"

Charley turned and ran back in the direction from which he came, "Davis, hang on. There's help on the way, hang on." But he feared it was too late.

***

Almost three months had passed since the horrible day at Spring Bank. It was 8:30 a.m. at the Little Rock Café on a Friday, the date of Davis Morgan's birth. Friends were there to mark the day and honor the man. Charley Nelson was in uniform, for when he left the celebration, he would return to his work. Charley was discovering that a chief's hours were not nine to five, and as the youngest police chief in the state, he felt as if he would be required to prove himself for some time. His new wife, Tonya, was at his side. Just three weeks earlier, they moved into Miss Helen's house when she relocated to an assisted living facility in Rome. They were having the time of their lives restoring their home, one room at a time. With their work schedules, it might take them years to get everything just the way they wanted it, but that was okay. They were having fun. It took Charley a while, but he finally learned that life is far better for the one who slows down to take one day at a time.

Amy and Jay sat at the table next to the young police chief and his wife. Amy lovingly held two-month-old Davis Morgan Archer who many people insisted looked a great deal like his grandfather. Jay beamed with pride and could not stop repeatedly glancing at his son. Jay and Amy were rapidly discovering the joys as well as the hardships of being parents and they loved every minute of it.

All the Little Rock gang were, of course, present. It was pretty much their show, planned and arranged by them. It was one of the first times in a long while that Brenda was not in work uniform at this hour. Today, she was not a waitress, but a guest. She sat beside Janie with Janie's mom on the other side. Janie had worked hard for the past month or two to have a better relationship with her mother, and she was pleased that the effort seemed to be paying off. She had heard Davis say several times that people usually treat you as you treat them. She had just about decided it wasn't simply a catchy saying, but an effective principle.

When his wife finally rolled the guest of honor through the door, the people around the crowded tables stood to their feet and applauded before they sang *For He's a Jolly Good Fellow*. Davis, both gratified and embarrassed by the attention, flashed a rather unnatural looking smile. Deidre earlier, told him the guys at the Little Rock wanted him to have breakfast with them on his birthday. He didn't suspect the entire dining room would be reserved for the occasion. Regardless of the reason, it was a treat for him to be out and about. Davis spent several weeks in the Floyd County Medical Center, where doctors first labored to keep him alive and then to perform delicate surgery to remove a bullet that went through his abdomen and lodged at the base of his spine. The result of that was the necessity for the wheel chair in which he was sitting. He spent days in therapy but was in only the beginning stages of learning to use the special leg braces and crutches that would allow him to get about on his own two feet. The doctors told him, he would never walk normally again, but he decided early on that he would show them. Nothing important had changed. God was still in charge.

There were friends who told him how unfortunate he was. He certainly wasn't fond of the pain and the sudden unpleasant changes that came to his life because of a freak chain of events. Sometimes he found himself vigorously objecting to his current situation, but then he understood that life, regardless of the circumstances, is always a challenge. He considered himself fortunate. No, not fortunate but blessed. He was alive. That was more than could be said for Chief Hanson who was ready to blast him to kingdom come if the Rat-Face Man had not shown up and took that shot. Davis didn't know if it were true, but he heard it said that Hanson's wound should not have killed him. The sad story was he had no desire to live and spend the rest of his life in prison or maybe even face the death penalty. Davis considered himself to be in a far better position than Clive Garrett who had survived but was now back in prison with his freedom taken from him again.

Yes, he was blessed because he would have a while longer with those he loved. He was a free man and paralysis affected only his legs. Others had much more than he with which to contend. Soon he would be back in his bookstore, and Charley insisted he continue as department chaplain. Deidre wasn't entirely pleased with that arrangement, but she was more tolerant of the idea when he promised her, his role would consist of only spiritual matters. His Jeep was in the process of being equipped with hand controls that would allow him to continue to drive it. What more could he ask for?

Davis remembered that Dean Nelson once threw-up in anticipation of presenting a two-minute speech in class when they were in middle school. Despite any past anxiety over such assignments, today Dean was proud to MC this birthday bash for his longtime friend.

Several of Davis's friends gave testimonials that made the event sound more like a roast than a birthday celebration. They sang a rousing rendition of *Happy Birthday* that could be heard down at City Hall.

"I believe it only fair the birthday boy be given a little rebuttal time," Dean announced. "Just remember, Davis, this isn't sermon hour at church. We've got to get out of here in time for the lunch crowd to be fed."

"Thank you, Dean. "I'm the most blessed man in the world to have so many friends like you people along with the best family a man could have." Davis looked first toward Deidre and then in the direction of Amy and Jay. "Today's number forty-eight for me, and I'm here to tell you it's been an eventful forty-eight years." Those around the tables laughed. "The Lord continues to bless me in so many ways, I cannot keep count of them all. As many of you know, one of my favorite scriptures is Psalm 1. It consists of only six verses, and I think I can quote them for you. This is the kind of man I'll continue to strive and struggle to be. I hope you'll join me in that effort.

"Blessed is the one who does not walk in step with the wicked or stand in the way that sinners take or sit in the company of mockers, but whose delight is in the law of the Lord, and who meditates on his law day and night. That person is like a tree planted by streams of water, which yields its fruit in season and whose leaf does not wither—whatever they do prospers.

Not so the wicked! They are like chaff that the wind blows away. Therefore the wicked will not stand in the judgment, nor sinners in the assembly of the righteous.

For the Lord watches over the way of the righteous, but the way of the wicked leads to destruction."

"I know I'll be in big trouble with my wife for sharing this last bit of information, but I can't help it. It's too good to keep to myself. We not only visited my doctor yesterday, we went to Deidre's doctor as well, and he confirmed it. Deidre is approximately three months pregnant. The Lord just keeps on blessing. I can't imagine what could top this surprise, but I've learned never to underestimate Him." The group of family and friends stood to their feet and applauded while Deidre with a wide smile first covered her face with both hands before removing them to mouth to the wonderful people before her words that came straight from her heart, I love you!

AFTERWORD

And so, we come to the end of the last Davis Morgan Mystery with mixed emotions. Writing these four stories gave us opportunity to get acquainted with Davis, Deidre, Charley, Amy, and the rest of the supporting cast. They have become part of our lives, and we will miss them. We trust they served their purpose regarding you, which was, first, to entertain and secondly, to highlight some important spiritual principles.

A third reason for the series was to serve as a learning tool for us. Having written only non-fiction in the past, we wanted to do Christian fiction. We concluded that mysteries with a message set in our home town would be a good way to learn the craft. We cringe a bit when we go back and look at the self-published first book in the series, not because of the story or characters, but because it reveals how little we knew about creating fiction. We graciously received traditional contracts from CrossLink Publishing for the three books that followed. Rick Bates and the CrossLink family have been extremely patient with us as we have endeavored to learn. I don't know that the stories got any better as we progressed through the series, but we acquired bushels of new knowledge about the craft. We want to use the experience we gained to continue to compose Christian fiction.

At this writing, we have not yet decided about our next project, not even the genre. We may continue with mystery because we love doing it. We may even come up with a new cast of characters set in Adairsville, with some of the characters from the

Davis Morgan series reoccurring. We have some other ideas that would take us in a completely different direction.

Thank you for your response to Davis and his friends. It has been gratifying. You have encouraged us to continue with our dreams.

We still reside in Adairsville, and would love for you to stop by and visit. Perhaps we will run into you at the 1902 Stock Exchange or Carol's General Store & Mercantile. We hang out a lot in those places. There is even talk that Davis Morgan will soon become the central focus in a dinner theater production. If you meet Wanda on your visit, talk nice to her, and she might include you in one of her Davis Morgan tours. We would love for you to stay in contact through our website: www.pelfreybooks.com.